Also by Kobo Abé

The Box Man

by KOBO ABÉ

Translated from the Japanese by
E. DALE SAUNDERS

Charles E. Tuttle Company
Suido 1-chome, 2-6, Bunkyo-ku, Tokyo

The Box Man

CLEAN SWEEP OF UENO HOBOS
Check This Morning—180 Arrests

During the predawn hours of the twenty-third, the Tokyo Ueno Police began to arrest those vagrants trying to avoid the cold of the approaching winter by camping in and around the underground passages of the Keisei Line, Ueno Railway Station, Ueno Park, Daito Ward, in the hopes of preventing further shootings by the long-sought criminal no. 109. A total of 180 persons were arrested in the underground passages and behind the Tokyo Institute of Culture, located within the Park precincts. They were arrested on the spot under the Law of Minor Offenses (infringement of the prohibition against loitering and vagrancy) and the Traffic Laws (acts prohibited on highways). All were taken to the Ueno Police Station, where they were photographed and fingerprinted. Four, who complained of being sick, were sent to the hospital via the Daito Welfare Office; nine were sent to a home for the aged. Those remaining were released after signing an agreement not to relapse into vagrancy. An hour later there was every indication that almost all had returned to their former haunts.

My Case

This is the record of a box man.

I am beginning this account in a box. A cardboard box that reaches just to my hips when I put it on over my head.

That is to say, at this juncture the box man is me. A box man, in his box, is recording the chronicle of a box man.

Instructions for Making a Box

MATERIALS:

1 empty box of corrugated cardboard
Vinyl sheet (semitransparent)—twenty inches square
Rubber tape (water-resistant)—about eight yards
Wire—about two yards
Small pointed knife (a tool)

> (*To have on hand, if necessary: Three pieces of worn canvas and one pair of work boots in addition to regular work clothes for streetwear.*)

Any empty box a yard long by a yard wide and about four feet deep will do. However, in practice, one of the standard forms commonly called a "quarto" is desirable. Standard items are easy to find, and most commercial articles that use standard-sized boxes are generally of irregular shape—various types of foodstuffs precisely adaptable to the container—so that the construction is sturdier than others. The most important reason to use the standardized form is that it is hard to distinguish one box from another. As far as I know, most box men utilize this quarto box. For if the box has any striking features to it, its special anonymity will suffer.

Even the common variety of corrugated cardboard has recently been strengthened, and since it is semiwaterproof there is no need to select any special kind unless you are going through the rainy season. Ordinary cardboard has better ventilation and is lighter and easier to use. For those who wish to occupy one box over a period of time, regardless of the season, I recommend the Frog Box, especially good in wet weather. This box has a vinyl finish, and as the name suggests, it is exceedingly strong in water. When new it has a sheen as if oiled, but apparently it produces static electricity easily, quickly absorbs dirt, and gets covered with dust; then the edge is thicker than the ordinary one and looks wavy. You can tell it at once from the common box.

To construct your box there is no particular procedure to follow. First decide what is to be the bottom and the top of the box—decide according to whatever design there may be or make the top the side with the least wear or just decide arbitrarily—and cut out the bottom part. In cases where one has numerous personal effects to carry, the bottom part can be folded inward without cutting, and, with wire and tape, the two ends can be made into a baggage rack. Tape the exposed part of the edges at the three points on the ceiling and at the one on the side where they come together.

The greatest care must be taken when making the observation window. First decide on its size and location; since there will be individual variations, the following figures are purely for the sake of reference. Ideally, the upper edge of the window will be six inches from the top of the box, and the lower edge eleven inches below that; the width will be seventeen inches. After you have subtracted the thickness of the base to stabilize the box when in place (I put a magazine on my head), the upper edge of the window comes to the eyebrows. You may perhaps consider this to be too low, but one seldom gets the opportunity to look up, while the lower edge is used frequently. When you are in an upright position, it will be difficult to walk if a stretch of at least five feet is not visible in front. There are no special grounds for computing the width. These parts should be adjusted to the required ventilation and the lateral strength of the box. At any rate since you can see right down to the ground, the window should be as small as possible.

Next comes the installation of the frosted vinyl curtain over the window. There's a little trick here too. That is, the upper edge is taped to the outside of the opening and the rest left to hang free, but please do not forget to anticipate a lengthwise slit. This simple device is useful beyond all expectations. The slit should be in the center, and the two flaps should overlap a fraction of an inch. As long as the box is held vertical, they will serve as screens, and no one will be able to see in. When the box is tilted slightly, an opening appears, permitting you to see out. It is a simple but extremely subtle contrivance, so be very careful when selecting the vinyl. Something rather heavy yet flexible is desirable. Anything cheap that immediately stiffens with temperature changes will be a problem. Anything flimsy is even worse. You need something flexible yet heavy enough not to have to worry about every little draft; the breadth of the opening can be easily regulated by tilting the box. For a box man the slit in the vinyl is comparable, as it were, to the expression of the eyes. It is wrong to consider this aperture as being on the same level as a peephole. With very slight adjustments it is easy to express yourself. Of course, this is not a look of kindness. The worst threatening glare is not so offensive as this slit. Without exaggeration, this is one of the few self-defenses an unprotected box man has. I should like to see the man capable of returning this look with composure.

In case you're in crowds a lot, I suppose you might as well puncture holes in the right and left walls while you're about it. Using a thickish nail, bore as many openings as possible in an area of about six inches in diameter, leaving enough space between them so the strength of the cardboard isn't affected. These apertures will serve as both supplementary peepholes and be convenient for distinguishing the direction of sounds. However unsightly, it will be more advantageous in case of rain to open the holes from the inside out and have the flaps facing out.

Last of all, cut the remaining wire into one-, two-, four-, and six-inch lengths, bend back both ends, and prepare them as hooks for hanging things on the wall. You should restrict your personal effects to a minimum; as it is, it's quite exhausting to arrange the indispensable items: radio, mug, thermos, flashlight, towel, and small miscellaneous bag.

As for the rubber boots, there's nothing particular to add. Just as long as they don't have any holes. If the canvas is wrapped around the waist, it is excellent for filling the space between oneself and the box and for holding the box in place. With three layers, divided in front, it is easy to move in all ways as well as being most convenient for defecation and urinating and for sundry other purposes.

An Example: The Case of A

Just making the box is simple enough; at the outside it takes less than an hour. However, it requires considerable courage to put the box on, over your head, and get to be a box man. Anyway, as soon as anyone gets into this simple, unprepossessing paper cubicle and goes out into the streets, he turns into an apparition that is neither man nor box. A box man possesses some offensive poison about him. I suppose there's some degree of poison even in a picture of the snake lady on a billboard or the bear man in a circus side show, but even so that can be canceled out by the admission fee. But the poison of a box man is not so simple.

For example, in your case, I'm sure you've not yet heard of a box man. Though there can't be any statistics, there is evidence that a rather large number of them are living in concealment throughout the country. But I've never heard that box men are being talked about anywhere. Evidently the world intends to keep its mouth tightly shut about them.

Have you ever actually seen one?

Let's stop fooling each other now. Certainly a box man is hardly conspicuous. He is like a piece of rubbish shoved between a guardrail and a public toilet or underneath a footbridge. But that's different from being inconspicuous or invisible. Since he is not especially uncommon, there is every opportunity of seeing one. Surely, even you have, at least once. But I also realize full well that you don't want to admit it. You're not the only one. Even with no ulterior motive, apparently one instinctively averts one's eyes. Yes, I suppose if you were to wear dark glasses at night or put on a mask, you couldn't help being considered some very timid creature or if not that, someone up to no good. All the more so then with a box man, who conceals his whole body; one can hardly object if he is considered suspicious.

Why, I wonder, would anyone deliberately want to be a box man? Perhaps you think it strange, but there are many amazing cases that explain why—trifling motivations that at first glance are not motivations at all. A is a case in point.

One day a box man took up residence directly below the window of A's apartment. Though A tried his best not to look, he did. No matter how he struggled to ignore the box man, he was very much aware of his presence. The first feelings that assailed A were anger and abhorrence toward a foreign body that has imposed itself, irritation and perplexity at having his territory encroached on illegally. But he decided to try and wait things out in silence for the time being. Anyway, he thought the neighborhood busybody, nagging about the garbage disposal or who knows what, would take action. But there was no sign that anybody was about to handle the matter. Unable to put up with the situation any longer, he complained to the janitor of the apartment building; but in vain. The box man was only visible from A's window, and anyone who could manage not to be seen would not deliberately move. As frequently as possible everybody pretended not to see him.

Finally A went to the police box himself. When the bored officer told him to fill out a damage report, A said that for the first time he experienced something similar to fear.

"Look here," the officer had snapped. "I suppose you made it clear he was to get out."

There was nothing for A to do but take action himself. On the way home from the police box he stopped at a friend's house and borrowed an air rifle. Once back in his room, he had a cigarette and calmed down; then he looked directly out the window, and as he did so the box man turned the observation slit of the box straight toward him. There were scarcely three or four yards between them. As if perceiving A's inner confusion, the box tilted, and the semiopaque vinyl curtain over the window divided vertically in two. From within, an indistinct whitish eye was firmly fixed on him. A felt a rush of blood go to his head. He flung open the window, and loading the gun, took aim.

But at what? At such close distance he might get the box man in the eye. And if he did that, it would only be trouble later on. It would be enough to shoot him somewhere else just to teach him not to show his face around here again. As A was speculating about his opponent's position in the box and the contours of his body, his finger, still on the trigger, began to grow numb and falter. It would be so much better if the fellow would vacate the premises because of a simple threat. He didn't want a single drop of blood left behind. But he couldn't wait forever. If a simple threat didn't work, it would be useless to try it again. He drew a bead. Again anger welled up within him. Time overheated, burned. He squeezed the trigger. The barrel of the gun, and then the box, made a noise like that of a wet trouser cuff snapped by an umbrella handle.

At the same time, the box gave a big leap. However inventively it may be used, corrugated cardboard is, after all, merely paper. Although it demonstrates considerable strength against general surface pressure, it is weak when stressed at a given point. The lead bullet must have bored into the fellow's body with great force. But neither the screams nor the jeers he had anticipated were forthcoming. Once it had leaped up, the box, again in repose, showed signs within of an extremely slow movement. A was at a loss. He had aimed several inches below and to the left of the line connecting the lower left and the upper right angles of the window. He estimated it to be about where the arm meets the right shoulder. Had he hesitated so long that his aim had deflected? But the box's reaction had been too great for that. An unpleasant thought occurred to him. The man in the box did not necessarily have to be facing front. The lower part of his body was completely covered with canvas, so there was no way to tell exactly what position he was in. He might have been sitting cross-legged, his knees on a diagonal in the box. If so, the bullet might well have grazed the top of the shoulder and hit the carotid artery.

An uncomfortable numbness formed an oval round A's mouth. Running steps in a dream. With bated breath A waited for the next movement. The box man did not budge. No, he had . . . he was clearly moving. The inclination was definitely increasing not so fast as the second hand of a watch but faster than the minute hand. Was he going to fall over? From the box came a sound like scraping on not fully dry clay. Suddenly the box man arose. He was unexpectedly tall. A heard a sound like that of striking a wet tent. Slowly changing his direction, the box man gave a low cough and stretched. He began to walk, swinging the box slightly right and left. The position of his hips was alarmingly toward the back, perhaps because he was bending forward. A thought the box had spoken, but he could not catch the words. When it got to the street that ran along the building, it disappeared around the corner in the same position. What disappointed A most of all was that he hadn't been able to see the expression on the box man's face.

Perhaps it was his imagination, but to A the surface of the ground behind the fleeing box man appeared darker than elsewhere. Five cigarette stubs had been snuffed out underfoot. An empty bottle was plugged with paper. Two enormous spiders were crawling about inside. One looked like a corpse. Crumpled wrapping paper from a chocolate bar. Then three large, successive blackish stains as big as a thumb. Were they blood stains? he wondered. No, phlegm or spittle doubtlessly. A simpered slightly as if in apology. Well, then, he had hit the target.

In about half a month, A had almost begun to forget the box man. But he was worried about using the shortcut to the station when he went to work, and to avoid the narrow lane, he unconsciously changed his route. Yet he still continued to look out of his window as soon as he woke up and first thing when he came home. If only he had not decided to turn in his icebox, in due course he would have been cured of this habit, but . . .

The new refrigerator, equipped with a freezing compartment, was normal enough, and it came in a corrugated cardboard box. Furthermore, it was just the right size. As soon as the contents were out and it was empty, A began to think of the box man. He heard the whipping sound again. He felt as if the air-rifle bullet had ricocheted from two weeks before. A was confused and decided at once to dispose of the box. But instead he washed his hands, blew his nose, and with great diligence, gargled repeatedly. The rebounding bullet flying about inside his cranium would doubtless set his brain functions askew. After observing the neighborhood for a while, he drew the curtains over the windows and gingerly crawled into the box.

Inside it was dark, and there was the sweet smell of waterproof paint. The place seemed very homelike. A recollection was on the verge of dawning, but he could not grasp it. He wanted to stay like this forever, but in less than a minute he came to his senses and crawled out. Feeling a little uneasy, he decided to keep the box for a while.

The following day, when he returned from work, A cut an observation window in the box with a knife, smiling bitterly, and then tried putting it on over his head like the box man. But he took it off immediately—he might well smile bitterly! He didn't understand what was happening. He viciously and resolutely kicked the box into a corner of the room, but not hard enough to destroy it.

On the third day he more or less regained his composure and tried looking out of the observation window. He couldn't recall what had surprised him so the evening before. He could definitely feel a change, but such a degree of change was desirable. From the whole scene, thorns fell and things appeared smooth and round. Stains on the wall with which he was completely familiar and which were utterly harmless to him . . . old magazines piled helter-skelter . . . a little television set with bent antennae . . . empty tins of corn beef beginning to overflow with cigarette butts . . . he was again made forcibly aware of the unconscious tension in himself by everything being so unexpectedly filled with thorns. Perhaps he should put aside his useless prejudice about boxes.

The next day A watched television with the box over his head.

From the fifth day on, except for sleeping, eating, defecating, and urinating, he lived in the box as long as he was in his room. Other than a twinge of conscience, he was not especially aware of doing anything abnormal. To the contrary, he felt that this was much more natural, he was much more at home. Even in the bachelor's life he had reluctantly led until now, misfortune had turned into blessing.

Sixth day. At length the first Sunday came around. He expected no visitors and had no place to go. From morning on, he stuck to the box. He was calm and relaxed, but something was missing. At noon he finally realized what he required. He went into town and bustled around making purchases: chamber pot, flashlight, thermos, picnic set, tape, wire, hand mirror, seven poster colors, plus various foodstuffs that could be eaten without preparation. When he got home he reinforced the box with the tape and the wire, and then, storing away the other items, he shut himself up in it. A hung the hand mirror on the inner wall of the box—left side toward the window—and then by the radiance of the flashlight he painted his lips green with one of the poster colors. After that he traced, in gradually expanding circles, the seven colors of the rainbow, beginning with red, around his eyes. His face resembled that of a bird or a fish rather than that of a man. It looked like the scene of an amusement park viewed from a helicopter. He could see his small retreating figure scampering off in it. There was no makeup so suitable to a box. Ultimately, he thought, he would become the contents that was right for the container. For the first time he casually masturbated in the box. For the first time he slept, leaning against the wall with the box over his head.

Then the following morning—just a week had gone by —A went stealthily out into the streets with the box over his head. And didn't come back.

If A made any error it was only that he was a little more overly aware of box men than others were. You cannot laugh at A. If you are one of those who have dreamed of, described in their thoughts even once, the anonymous city that exists for its nameless inhabitants, you should not be indifferent, because you are always exposed to the same dangers as A—that city where doors are opened for anyone; where even among strangers you need not be on the defensive; where you can walk on your head or sleep by the roadside without being blamed; where you are free to sing if you're proud of your ability; and where, having done all that, you can mix with the nameless crowds whenever you wish.

Thus it will seldom do to point a gun at a box man.

A Safety Device . . . Just in Case

Now I may seem to be repeating myself, but I am at present a box man. And for a while I intend to write about me.

I am getting along here with these notes, as I take shelter from the rain under a bridge. Overhead the Prefectural Highway Three crosses a canal. It is just fifteen or sixteen minutes past nine by my not too accurate watch. The dark night sky trails its skirt of rain low over the surface of the land. It has been falling since morning. Fishery warehouses and lumber sheds stretch away as far as the eye can see. There are no human habitations and no one passes by. Even the headlights of trucks coming and going on the bridge do not reach this far. A flashlight suspended from the ceiling lights the paper beneath my hand. Perhaps that is why the letters formed by my ballpoint pen seem almost black when they should be green.

The seaside smell of rain is quite like a dog's breath. The place is not all that suitable as a rain shelter, for the drizzle is directionless as if expelled from an atomizer. The bridge girders are too high. This entire location is unsuitable. Everything —being at a place like this at a time like this—is unnatural and not like a box man. For example, using an electric flashlight is a terrible waste. People like us, who live on the road, make do almost completely with items we pick up from the streets. It is an extravagance to use an electric flashlight only for the purpose of writing notes. With the number of new streetlamps there's plenty of light to read a newspaper while taking shelter from the rain.

Somehow it's been over two hours since I sat myself down in this spot so ill-suited to a box man. But I should begin with an explanation. Of course, no matter how diligent I am with my justifications, I am not confident of completely convincing you. Anyway you won't believe them. But the truth's the truth and that's that. This box of mine has been sold to someone. There is a buyer willing to pay fifty thousand yen. I'm waiting for her now to make the transaction. If you find it incredible, I too am suspended between belief and disbelief. There's no way of believing, is there. I don't understand the reason for someone wanting to pay out good money for an old worn-out paper box.

Why did I react to such a temptation when I didn't believe the buyer was serious? The reason is simple. There was no reason to be suspicious, that's all. It's just like being stopped by a shining object on the side of the road. My buyer was shining like a piece of broken beer bottle in the evening sun. One knows it is of no value, but there is nonetheless a strange fascination with the light refracted by the glass. One is unexpectedly made to feel as if one were seeing another time dimension. Her legs especially were as delicate and graceful as the rails of a railroad seen from an eminence, stretching away into the distance. Bluish, light steps where, like the open skies, nothing obstructs the line of vision. There was no reason for believing her, but neither was there reason to doubt her. It was as if, without realizing it, I had been completely disarmed by her legs.

Of course, I am remorseful now. Or rather it may be better to say that I am absolutely depressed by the premonition that I shall be made to feel serious remorse. A wretched feeling. No matter how I think about it, it is not like a box man. It is as if I have abandoned the prerogatives of a box man. If there is hope, it is so subtle as to be undetectable even with a high-energy analyzer. Is some transformation beginning to take place in' my box? Perhaps so. On reflection, after wandering about this town, I have the feeling that the surface of the box has become fragile and terribly vulnerable. Certainly the town bears me some ill will.

Of course, choosing this place was partially the buyer's idea, even though I did suggest it. My danger is her danger. At the foot of the bridge stands a stone Jizo, the guardian of dead children, with a red flannel bib, apparently placed there in memory of some child who died by drowning. There is a recently painted white sign beside a flight of stone steps that leads down to a boat landing slightly upstream, prohibiting playing in the water. But fortunately the vinyl over the ob-

servation window has been moistened by the rain, and because of the faded matting effect, the visibility is enhanced.
The concrete embankment along the canal cuts diagonally in
bold relief across the window. The wan lights of a small
freighter at berth, wavering fractionally against the current,
spill over palely onto the sidewalk at the top of the embankment, and if someone were to pass by he would be as conspicuous as a spot of ink on clothing.

There! A cat cut directly across the pavement. A stray
cat with a filthy matted coat. It is manifestly pregnant and
has a bulging white belly heavy with its load of kittens. Its
tattered ears bear the marks of fighting. And since I can distinguish such details, even as my pen glides along, perhaps I
need not be neurotic. No matter what, the buyer, even if she
wants to, won't be able to take me by surprise all that easily.

Of course, what I want most of all is for her to come
here of her own accord as she promised. But as you see, too
much is vague. I can't understand—fifty thousand yen for
this box—and why would she want to negotiate in a place
like this? There's no reason to believe her, nor is there any to
doubt her. There's no reason to doubt, nor is there to believe.
A slender transparent, ephemeral neck. Anyway there's nothing better than being on my guard. Hence my little safety
device. If worst comes to worst, I intend to leave these notes
as evidence. Whatever death I meet, I have no desire for suicide. If I die it won't be suicide even by mistake, but definitely foul play. No matter how much one rejects the world
and disappears from it by getting into a box, essentially a box
is di . . .

> (Stop. Out of ink. I get an old pencil from my
> bag. Two and a half minutes to sharpen it. For-
> tunately I have not yet been killed. As proof, I
> have changed from a ballpoint pen to a pencil, but
> my writing is exactly the same as before.)

Now what is it I started to write? The last thing I wrote was perhaps the first letters of "different." Perhaps I meant to write: "A box man is different from a vagrant," or something like that. Of course, as far as society is concerned they apparently don't distinguish very clearly between the two, as much as box men do. Indeed, they have not a few points in common. For example, not having an I.D. card, or a profession, or an established place of residence, or indication of name or age, or a set time or place for eating and sleeping. And then not getting your hair cut or brushing your teeth, rarely taking a bath, needing almost no cash for daily living, and a lot of other things.

Yet, beggars and vagrants are apparently quite aware of a difference. Any number of times they made me feel unpleasant. Sometime when I have the opportunity I intend to write about it, but the Wappen beggars are especially offensive to me. The minute I draw near the beggars' and vagrants' area they make me experience a reaction close to morbid nervousness that is a far cry from indifference. I am looked at with more undisguised contempt and hostility than by anyone who pays his daily expenses and lives at a recorded address. I have, in fact, never heard of a beggar turning into a box man. Since I have no intention of being a beggar, he has none of being a box man. Even so I do not intend to look down on them. Surprisingly enough, even beggars are a part of the environs that belong to the townsfolk, and when you become a box man perhaps you're below a beggar.

Paralysis of the heart's sense of direction is the box man's chronic complaint. At such times the axis of the earth sways, and one suffers a severe nausea resembling seasickness. But for some reason there is absolutely no relationship with the consciousness of being a social dropout. Not once does he feel guilty about the box. I personally feel that a box, far from being a dead end, is an entrance to another world. I don't know to where, but an entrance to somewhere, some other world. I say this, but the opening to that other world is not very different from a dead-end alley if I stifle my nausea as I examine the world outside my little observation window. Let's stop using the fancy words. I mean I don't yet have any desire to die.

Yet it's too late. Indeed I wonder if she intends to renege on her promise. I still have seven matches. Wet tobacco is absolutely tasteless.

Promises . . . promises . . .

To take away the bitter taste, a drop of whiskey. A little less than a third left in my pocket flask.

But it's all right if she doesn't come. Is breaking a promise anything to get excited about? I'll be a lot more amazed if she puts in an appearance as she said she would. What if she doesn't go back on her promise but sends a substitute in her place? And I'm positive this will happen. A substitute will come in her place. I have a general idea as to who that will be, too. In the final analysis they are both in it together. With her as decoy, the substitute intends to lure me under the bridge as a place of execution. Since I am a born victim— indeed, as I am a box man, which is the same as not existing, no matter how they try they'll never kill me—the role of killer automatically goes to my enemy. That doesn't mean that everything proceeds according to logic. I'm prepared to meet the attack. The wet surface of the slope is steep and slippery. Of course, when it comes to strength, I fancy he has something of an edge on me. I wonder if, contrary to my feelings, deep down I don't want to die.

Now, then, time and place are suitable to the victim. The speed of the tide is ideal too. A very old-fashioned thick-bodied bridge that spans like a last constricting ring the funnel-shaped mouth of the canal swollen at high tide with sea water. As the central portion rises in an arc to let ships pass, the girders from the area at the foot of the bridge are conspicuously high. Since I am a box man walking around with a waterproofed room on my back like a snail, there is no need to worry about mere rain blown sideways or the height of girders. Compared to a real room the weak point of a box is that it has no floor, I suppose. If the wet wind comes blowing up from underneath, it is hard to avoid, whatever I do. But you can think of it in another light: precisely because there is no flooring, I can sit close by the water's edge without fear of being flooded. Even if the water level suddenly rises, swollen at high tide by the rain, as long as it doesn't exceed the height of my boots I can always stand up and change positions. For those who have not actually had the experience, this will seem madly carefree. Besides from now on the tide will be going out. No need to worry lest the water rise more than it has. The black band of seaweed, as if drawn with a ruler along the base of the embankment now rotting from oil wastes, clearly divides the view into upper and lower parts.

A dark swell spreading out from somewhere has begun to erase the ripples from the surface of the water. Immediately downstream from the bridge pylons, large and small whirlpools, sluggish, like the melting of unrefined rice honey, gradually begin to form. They are actually rather small depressions; but wooden fish boxes, fragments of bamboo baskets, and plastic containers draw falteringly near, swirl suddenly around, trembling, turn over several times, and just as their speed seems to slacken, are all at once swallowed up.

Yes, indeed, in an emergency I shall join these notes to the wooden boxes and the bamboo baskets. The shadow of someone appears on the embankment; if it is not she, I shall immediately put them in a vinyl bag, seal the mouth after blowing it up, and wrap the opening several times with the thin wire that I have doubled. About twenty-two to twenty-three seconds. Then I shall bind red vinyl tape over the wire, leaving long conspicuous ends. I shall fix a stone, the size of a fist, to the tape by means of twisted paper. That will take less than five seconds. The whole business will take about thirty seconds. However long it lasts, it shouldn't take more than one minute. Furthermore, no matter how her substitute hurries it will take him two to three minutes to come down the stone stairway by the landing, cross the slippery stone slope, and get here. I have no fear I won't have plenty of time. If he shows the slightest strange behavior, I shall immediately throw the bag into the current. It should go pretty far with the attached stone. No matter how he tries to reach it, he'll never get it. The bag will head directly toward the whirlpools. If he's an expert swimmer I wonder if he'll plunge in and chase after it? No, an expert would surely avoid such recklessness. Even the passage of small boats is forbidden after the tide has begun to withdraw. But he will be aware of the whirlpools without reading the sign on the embankment. After faltering for a while, the bag will ultimately be swept out to sea. Then after hours or days the paper string will come undone and the stone will be released. The air-filled bag will easily attract attention with its red tape, drifting in with the shore tides.

Thus if the man who shot me were to appear right now, according to the contents of the notes up to this point, he will be the one who tried to kill me. Impossible. Even if I specify his name here on this page, I doubt I can get anyone to believe me. If I try to explain the motives, I will simply weaken the credibility of the notes even more. It will all sound like a lie. But I've got my wits about me. I've attached a black-and-white negative with cellophane tape to the upper right-hand corner of the inside cover. Perhaps it is not very clear, but it will constitute absolutely unshakable evidence. It's the back view of a middle-aged man hurrying off, hiding his air rifle under his arm, the muzzle pointed downward along his body. When enlarged, I suppose you will be able to distinguish the various features even better. He is poorly dressed, but the cloth is strong and of excellent quality. Yet the trousers are full of creases. His fingers are heavy and solid, but the tips are rounded and look as if they have never experienced work. And then the fancy shoes are most conspicuous. They are low shoes, like slippers, with the sides scooped out and the soles thin. He is in a profession in which he takes them off and puts them on more than the ordinary number of times.

These notes, if the finder so wishes, can make him a little fortune.

There! The whirlpools are beginning to swell. There is absolutely no need to worry about being seen. Heavy trucks piled high with frozen fish or pulpwood kick up the thick concrete slabs immediately above on the bridge, honking and crossing back and forth every few seconds; they are absorbed only in their own noise and are like blind beasts. This is an ideal place not only for the disposal of corpses but for living humans as well. And an ideal place for murder must be an ideal place to be murdered.

The lead in my pencil is gone. Come on, come on . . . I've had enough. Is she really going to come or not?

> (I can't sharpen the pencil with this rusty knife. Tomorrow, if I'm able to prolong my existence until then, I must get two or three ballpoint pens. The ones around the service entrance of the Middle School have the most ink left in them.)

Two or Three Additions Concerning the Photographic Evidence Attached to the Inner Cover

Time of shooting: One evening about a week or ten days ago (paralysis of the sense of time is one of the chronic ailments of a box man).

Place of shooting: The mountainside end of the long black wall of the soy-sauce factory (the shadow of the wall cuts diagonally across the foreground of the picture).

At the time I was just in the act of standing there relieving myself. Suddenly there was a sharp noise. It resembled the sound of a pebble kicked up by a truck striking the box (that frequently happened, for I often lay by the roadside). But no truck, not to mention any three-wheeled conveyance, had passed by. At the same time a sharp pain like biting down on ice with a bad tooth pierced my left shoulder, and my urine stopped flowing. Looking out the little hole in the side, I saw the sweeping branches of an old mulberry tree just where the curve began along the sweet potato field of the hatchery and where the wall of the soy factory ended and became a slope and the pavement gave way to a graveled walk (a part is visible on the left side of the photo). Turning away from the shadow of the tree (that is, as if to run away), a man was beginning to get up. He shifted a sort of stick about three feet long from his shoulder and put it under his arm, whereupon it caught the evening sun and gleamed a reddish black. I at once concluded that it was an air rifle. Without rearranging myself after urinating, I set up my camera. (To tell the truth, before I became a box man I was a photographer who had just become independent. Since I had become a box man right in the midst of my career, for no particular reason I still went around with a minimum of photographic equipment.) Changing the direction of the box, I snapped three pictures in succession. (I did not have the time to regulate the distance, but as the camera was set at ƒ11 at one two-hundred-and-fiftieth of a second, it was more or less in focus.) The fellow sprang to the side, crossed the road, and disappeared from view.

Almost everything up until now can be proved by analyzing the film. But from this point on, nothing at all is backed by objective evidence. I expect that either you or the finder of these notes will believe my testimony and justify it on your own.

FIRST CONJECTURE CONCERNING THE TRUE CHARACTER OF THE SNIPER. I should like you to refer to the "Case of A." When someone is infected by the idea of a box man and tries himself to become one, there is a general tendency to overreact by shooting him with an air rifle. Thus I did not cry out for help or make any attempt at pursuit. Rather I thought that the candidates for box man had increased by one, and I experienced a feeling of closeness to him. Thereupon the pain in my shoulder receded and changed into a feeling of incandescence. From now on it was rather the sniper who must endure a pain a hundred times worse. There was no need to inflict any greater chastisement on him than this.

As I gazed at the deserted sloping road after the disappearance of the rifle man, I felt moist like a broken water faucet. The smoke that smelled like burnt sugar came from the soy factory and diligently filed away at the ends of the sharp shadows cast by the evening sun, dulling the angles. Somewhere in the distance, the monotonous grating of firewood being sawed. And still further in the distance, the lively sound of a racing motorbike engine. But after two or three seconds had gone by, there was no sign of anyone at all. Could it be that the inhabitants had withdrawn underground like grubs? A scene so calm that it induced an overwhelming desire to see a human being . . . anyone. But a box man's eyes cannot be deceived. Looking out from the box, he sees through the lies and secret intentions concealed behind the scenery. The scenery evidently intended to shake me up by pretending that this was a road where one could not go astray, intended for my surrender, but unfortunately I was not to be taken in. I just wanted to relieve myself at my leisure. The area around a station or a crowded shopping district was more suited to a box man. I liked the honesty of it. I felt at home with it— three or four straight roads pretending to be a labyrinth. For this reason I don't like provincial towns. Anyway there are too many sham straight roads there. Thinking of the confusion of the air-rifle man lost on such a road, I felt sentimental without meaning to.

As I pressed down on the wound, my fingers became sticky and covered with blood. Suddenly I was uneasy. It may be all right in one of the busier quarters of Tokyo, but in this commercial section of T City, there isn't room for two box men. If he insists on becoming a box man, it necessarily follows that a territorial dispute will be unavoidable. When he realizes he can't drive me out with an air rifle, it doesn't mean that he won't come for me next time with a shotgun. Was I wrong in the way I reacted? Frankly, fellows like him have tried to get on intimate terms with me any number of times.

One addressed me directly and even stopped me in the street. At the time, I looked back at him in silence from the crack in the inclined vinyl curtain. Anyone would have been nonplused at that. Even a policeman or a railway guard would have shrunk back. I wondered if I should have said something before I drove him to his air rifle.

BUT THE CONJECTURE HAS COMPLETELY CHANGED WITH A NEW CAST OF CHARACTERS . . . The new character in the cast came riding on a bicycle. As I was concentrating on the sham road, a voice suddenly came from behind me. "There's a hospital at the top of the slope," it said. White fingertips grazed the observation window, and three thousand-yen notes were tossed in. I felt like a mailbox and turned to see a retreating figure already some ten yards away. It was apparently a young girl whose low, rasping voice did not suit her. I had no time to point the camera in her direction, and she disappeared around the corner at the next lane. I had observed her for only a few seconds, yet I was quite taken by the movement of her legs propelling the bicycle. They were slender, but not too slender—light legs with a well-proportioned curve. The backs of her knees were glossy and beautiful like the inside of a shell. They were so vivid that I have no memory of the color of the dress she was wearing. But I wasn't necessarily disarmed. If by that evening, the wound in my shoulder had not worsened, I probably would not have made it a point to go to the hospital at the top of the slope. Nor would I have realized that the air-rifle man (as the photo clearly showed) was in fact the hospital doctor and the girl on the bicycle, the nurse. Furthermore, quite naturally, I should not have been in the ridiculous situation of waiting for her—or her substitute—in such a dangerous place under the bridge.

But I just put another cigarette to my lips. Again and again I counted over the thousand-yen notes and, folding them in three, I dropped them into one of my rubber boots. They say that a wild bird that has been captured will refuse food and die of hunger. But the condemned convict relishes his last cigarette. I, who was no bird, leisurely lit the cigarette, reflecting that there was no connection between the rifle man and the nurse. It made absolutely no difference; the rifle man was the rifle man and the girl the girl. It was all right to assume that her hurrying on ahead was an expression of her delicacy, that she was simply ashamed of her charitable act.

But no matter how much I chain-smoke, the executioner will not wait. Indeed the time for execution is drawing closer. By dawn the wound in my shoulder had begun to fester and the pain had constricted me like an overly narrow rubber tunnel. When I slipped out of the box, I found myself at the hospital at the top of the slope. The bicycle girl holding a hypodermic needle and the air-rifle man grasping a scalpel were waiting for me. Rather than being surprised by this turn of events, it seemed that I had been expecting it from the very beginning.

After a while I awoke in a bed; the bicycle girl was peering at me and there was a heavy smell of disinfectant and vitamins. Apparently the white nurse's uniform had the function of stopping time. When time stopped, the causal relationship among things was naturally interrupted; and no matter what indecent act I might commit, I had absolutely no fear of being blamed. Unfortunately, as a matter of fact, I was not relaxed enough to try anything indecent, but with the box off, I experienced such a sense of release that it made me forget that I was showing my naked face. With each random detail I told her about myself she smiled encouragingly, a smile hewn of solidified air, so transitory and yet so defenseless, as if colored with a brush of light, that I had the illusion of having been made a confession of love to. Her face was so wreathed in smiles that it even made me forget the fact that her legs were quite hidden by the overly low hemline of her uniform. I beat my wings like a little bird starting to fly for the first time (clumsily, incompetently, yet in a daze). Then my wings took the air—now I'm going to fly!—and intoxicated with her airy smile, I felt that I no longer need return to the box. Before I realized it I was making a promise I myself did not understand, a promise to buy the box for her for fifty thousand yen directly from the box man. I had had an acquaintance with box men (quite naturally); I even stressed that I would sell it to her for nothing. I thought I had best inquire on the spot just what she planned to do with it. But I was powerless before her smile. It seemed foolish even to discuss the uses of a box.

As soon as I had left the hospital, her smile vanished. When I returned to the place where I had concealed my box under the bridge, I began to have stomach spasms and vomited for some time. It seemed that I had been drugged without knowing it. Though at last I realized that I had apparently been taken in, I could not hate her.

> (Here a score or more lines of marginal addenda. The writing and, of course, the color of the ink are all but indistinguishable from those of the main text.)

—I'm talking about the beggar who wore a box over his head, she said.

—I know, because I'm a photographer. A photographer's a Peeping Tom. His specialty is boring holes . . . anywhere. By nature a churl . . .

—A worn-out cardboard box . . .

—I thought perhaps it was a friend of mine. I guess I was wrong. But I can't claim to be completely mistaken. A fellow photographer happened to take a picture of the box man without realizing it himself. Then he got interested and ran around chasing him all over, but he didn't run into him again. Instead, he got interested in photographing the town. The seamy side of town that has an aversion to being seen . . . and since he took pictures of what had an aversion to being seen, he was obliged to do it on the sly so that he wouldn't be noticed. It suddenly occurred to him to put on a box and go around taking pictures in the guise of a box man. Since he himself had not seen the box man when he had been looking straight at him, nobody would take any notice of *him* with a box on his head. In effect no one did seem to notice him, and he was able to take as many pictures as he wanted. He became a fake box man and threw himself into taking snapshots of the streets. But just as he was acquiring some reputation among his fellow photographers he suddenly vanished. Since then he has not returned to his apartment. Rumor has it that he has become a real box man.

—I wouldn't mind how much I was seen.

—But this kind of seeing is like shaving something off with a knife, like tearing off the clothes you're wearing.

—A long time ago I used to do modeling.

—Seriously, I'd like to do whatever I can. But I can't do anything. It's exasperating, but about the only thing I can manage is to squint through the range finder and snap the shutter. And then float your transparent image in the developer. The yellowish-green bulb that resembles fluorite . . . the second hand of the clock in the darkroom that indicates the position of eight . . . the surface of the water-repellent photographic paper that gleams like an oily membrane . . . the faint outline that gradually appears . . . an outline from which another appears . . . an outline superimposed on an outline . . . at length the contours of your naked body, like the footprints of some criminal imprinted in my heart . . .

—I want that box.

DEAD BY THE ROADSIDE
Ignored by 100,000 People

About seven o'clock in the evening of the twenty-third, members of the Shinjuku patrol discovered a forty-year-old vagrant dead, leaning against a pillar in the underground passage of the West Exit to Shinjuku Station, Tokyo, where people returning from work and shoppers were coming and going. According to the information provided by the same officials, the man was five feet two and of medium weight. He was wearing a long-sleeved shirt with a floral pattern and work boots; his hair was in the mussy style of a vagrant. Besides a hundred and twenty-five yen in change, he had only several sheets of newspaper, which he perhaps intended to use to sleep on. He possessed nothing else with which to establish his identity, place of residence, or name. Several hundreds of thousands of passengers a day frequent the underground passage in question (Shinjuku Station Report), and nearby there were many people and a line of public telephones. According to eyewitnesses, the man had remained sitting in the same position since noon that day, but no one had taken any notice of him, nor had he been reported for the six or seven hours before the police found him. Further, the man was scarcely ten yards from the police box, but the officer on duty said he was not visible on the other side of the pillar.

Then I Dozed Off
a Number of Times

I wonder if you've heard about shellweed. It may be this grass with thorny leaves like twists of firecrackers that covers the whole rocky slope where I am now sitting.

When you smell the fragrance of shellweed they say you dream of being a fish.

The story should be taken with a grain of salt, I feel, but it's not implausible. As shellweed prefers swampy land containing considerable salt, naturally it grows readily at the seashore, and it is not particularly surprising that there should be a tradition of its odor producing dreams of fish. Furthermore, according to one explanation, the alkaloids in its pollen bring about a floating sensation that resembles dizziness; and since at the same time it irritates the respiratory membranes, it is also possible, apparently, to have the hallucination of drowning in water.

But if that were all, it would not be particularly surprising. What's worrisome about a shellweed dream is not so much the dream itself as the problem of awakening from it. With a real fish there's no way of knowing, but they say that the passage of time that the dream fish experiences is quite different from when it is awake. The speed is remarkably slower, and one has the feeling that a few terrestrial seconds are drawn out to several days or several weeks.

Nevertheless, thanks to the strangeness of the dream scenery, one at first takes the utmost delight in the lightness of one's body, subtracted as it is from gravity, sporting among the undulating seaweed in the shadows of rocks, passing through strips of light limned by the lens of the waves, chasing after schools of trusting fish. As one is light oneself, one feels as if the world itself has become buoyant. One is completely liberated from bodily afflictions caused by gravity —drooping belly, stiffness of shoulders and neck, pain in the knee joints, falling arches—and one frolics around as if one were at least ten years younger. The lightness intoxicates the dream fish like alcohol.

But unless the fish is real, every case of intoxication sobers up and ultimately palls. In the sluggish flow of time, boredom soon becomes unbearable. It should not be too hard to imagine the feeling of irritation the completely bored dream fish experiences, the lack of resistance as if its five senses were numbed. Soon the free lightness of substance gradually begins to pall. One's whole body is wrapped round and round, as if forced into a restrictive garment in the shape of a fish. The soles of the feet send out feelers, seeking the sense of resistance they are used to when walking on land. The joints begin to recall fondly the heaviness of the various tissues and musculature that govern them. There is an unreasonable desire to walk. And suddenly one is amazed to realize that one lacks the legs necessary to do so.

But legs aren't the only thing lacking. No ears, no neck, no shoulders, and more than anything else, no arms. An inexpressible sense of deficiency. Quite definitely because the arms have been torn off. No curiosity can ultimately be satisfied unless one can check by touching with one's hands. If one wants really to know another person, if one does not know him with one's fingers, push him, punch him, bend him, tear at him, one can scarcely claim to know him completely. One wants to touch, to pass one's hands all over him. The bag of scales is insufferable for the fish. It strains to tear it off, but all it can do is to open its gills wide, raise its dorsal

If you intend to proceed beyond here, you either have to go over the fence or around it to the right or left. Since this area is the middle, whichever way you go around it takes the same amount of time. When walking, it usually takes a day and a half, but if you rest on the way it takes more.

fin rigid, and trail a cord several inches long of pepper-colored excrement.

Writhing in a pain that floods to the very tips of its toes, the sham fish suddenly arrives at the fatal suspicion that he is perhaps fake. The instant doubt begins, everything becomes very strange. When one has the body of a fish, without any vocal cords to begin with, to say nothing of hands or feet, one is plagued in one's use of such words. Double perception is as irritating as an itch.

Perhaps all such happenings are dream sequences.

Nevertheless, the dream is too long. It has been going on for so long that one can no longer remember when it started. However protracted, one will supposedly awaken from it sometime.

To ascertain that one is dreaming, the first thing—and it's reliable, for I have tried it several times myself—is to give the back of the hand a good pinch. But unfortunately a fish doesn't have nails to pinch with, nor a hand to pinch the back of. If that doesn't work, you can jump heroically from a steep cliff. That too I remember having succeeded at any number of times. Certainly if a fish is capable of that, there's no particular inconvenience in not having arms or legs. But what kind of a fall would a sea fish have?

I have never, of course, heard of a fish falling. Even a dead fish floats to the surface. It's much more complicated than a balloon falling in air. As far as the descent is concerned, it's a reverse fall. A reverse fall . . .

Indeed, does such a way of waking from a dream exist? I suppose a fish may well drown in air by falling in reverse, upward, toward the sky. The danger of death is the same. It's the same as a fall on land, and one of necessity awakens from the dream.

Yet once having pushed his thinking this far, the fake fish, with a timidity unexpected in a cold-blooded animal, still hesitates. They say that when one is able to realize that one is dreaming one is already near the end of the dream. The fish has done all he can do to wake up, and although it is waiting a while longer to see just what will happen, it will not influence the outcome.

The fake fish decided to wait. His very determination touched with the pallidness of the sea seemed to have paled.

Days, weeks passed, and the time had come for the fake fish to reach his decision. A storm had broken. A great tropical storm bore down, causing the bottom of the sea to tremble. Great waves rose, making the timid and indecisive fake fish demonstrate what little courage he had. But he was in no hurry to die. He simply gave himself over to the movement of the waves.

Suddenly a wave crest like the blades of fifty electric saws marshaled horizontally bore down on him. Sweeping the fake fish before it, it broke momentously against the cliffs and tossed the fish high into the air. And the fake fish drowned in the atmosphere.

Now I wonder if he awoke from his dream. No, one does not have a shellweed dream so casually. It is altogether different from an ordinary one. As the fake fish died before awakening, he could not expect to awaken from his dream again. He still had to go on dreaming until after he died. Ultimately the dead fake fish apparently would exist forever as a fake fish, as if it had received the latest freezing treatment. They say that among those fish tossed up onto the seashore after the storm there were not a few unlucky ones who had fallen asleep suffocated by the flowers of the shellweed.

But for some reason I have not yet become a fish. I have apparently dropped off any number of times, but I am still the box man I was. On reflection, a fake fish and a box man don't seem conspicuously different. The fake me becomes something not at all myself when I put on the box. Perhaps I who have been immunized against being something fake no longer possess the capability of having the dream of a fish. No matter how many times box men keep awakening from their dreams, they apparently end up being only the box men they always were.

The Promise Is Fulfilled, and a Letter with Fifty Thousand Yen Covering the Cost of the Box Was Dropped from the Top of the Bridge. This Was Barely Five Minutes Ago. I Attach the Letter Herewith.

I trust you. No receipt is required. As for the disposal of the box, I leave that up to you too. Before the tide goes out, tear it up and throw it into the sea.

. . .

Something strange has happened. I have read and reread her letter. Can there be some other way of interpreting it? At this point, I can only give a literal explanation. I try smelling the stationery with green lines that has been folded in three. It simply has the faint odor of disinfectant.

I assumed arbitrarily that the doctor would come. My various strategies all presupposed an attack by him. However, she herself was the one who came. Yes, she herself came. She came herself. She herself . . . the reason is quite unclear . . . oh, it's clear enough . . . she was simply carrying out her promise. I wonder why I am upset? Didn't I quite expect betrayal on her part? Perhaps so. A betraying woman like her quite suits me. I'll indeed be at a loss if the promise is kept. But just a minute, perhaps I have committed some important oversight. For example, I might well try rethinking her position . . . and her role in the affair.

> *I don't think there is any point in continuing writing. Since I have neither killed nor been killed, there's nothing further to explain.*
>
> *A letter adrift in space . . . address unknown . . . shall I tear it up and throw it away?*

Calm down now. Look here, fifty thousand yen. But since I have the money, simply disposing of the notes isn't enough. She wants me to dispose of the *box.* With the fifty thousand yen, its ownership has already passed to her. If I intend to respect her will, I suppose I shall have to dispose of it as I promised. Even so, I don't understand. Who in heaven's name would stand to gain by my doing such a thing? Fifty thousand yen just to throw the box into the sea—it's too much money. Am I so offensive? I must not flatter myself; by rights the motive must be something more practical. Some more matter-of-fact reason so that she should not feel she has lost something even in paying fifty thousand yen.

I don't understand it at all. It is just as well that I'm in a

fog. I wonder, should I insist on returning the fifty thousand?
She is sorely mistaken if she thinks I'm not capable of doing it.

But such an interpretation doesn't hold. It's a plan she
divised so the doctor wouldn't get the box. For some reason
he wanted it very much. Perhaps at first she too fell in with
his plan. Or else was pretending to. But as the time to carry
it out at last drew nearer, her doubts began to grow. Whatever she thinks, she can't believe anything good will come of
it. But no matter how she remonstrated with him, the doctor
turned a completely deaf ear, and in the end she could do
nothing but oppose him. Fortunately the box man seems to
have an uncommon affection for her. If she leaves the disposal of the box up to the box man himself and he disappears,
whatever the doctor may think up, she will be able to contain
him before he does anything.

Indeed . . . somehow I feel it makes sense . . . the
box may perhaps be worth fifty thousand yen, depending on
the doctor's reason for acquiring it. The circumstances are
totally different, depending on whether her motive for inter-
fering stems from her own selfishness or from a desire to
protect the doctor. But I recognize that at least there is a
conflict between them. And if that's true, then it's not a bad
sign.

However, I do not fancy disposing of the box as she
wishes. I still know too little about her to trust her. At least
I had better put off disposing of the box until I check her
real motives once more. I have the right to do that much.
And then, frankly speaking, I am dissatisfied. It's fine that
she herself put in an appearance, but it was altogether too
businesslike. She didn't even come down the embankment.
When she had sped past the "No Playing in the Water"
sign, mounted on a bicycle made of some light alloy and

equipped with five-speed gears—illuminated by the lights of a freighter, her raincoat gleamed as if gilded . . . through the fabric the outline of her body was clearly visible . . . and then the movement of those calves and knees which so disarmed me—she had gone out on the provincial highway, ignoring the frantic signals I flashed with my flashlight. After a while a trembling circle of light came slipping over the surface of the ground about two yards ahead of me. It was the beam of her flashlight shining between the balustrades of the bridge. I couldn't very well look up, it is too awkward for a box man. Then there was a sound, and not far from the trembling circle of light something fell. It was a vinyl bag weighted with a stone. In it were the letter in question and five ten-thousand-yen bills rolled up. She went off without doing anything else. While she had come as close to me as could be, she had gone off without saying a word. The movement of her calves disappeared into the darkness, the glitter of the wet raincoat vanished, and last of all the red taillight of the bicycle faded away. When I had read the letter and counted the bills, I suddenly began to hear the sound of drizzle, which should not have been audible. Perhaps it was the blood coursing in my head.

Fifty thousand yen. I should like to tell her alone that for the person paying out perhaps it is an extravagance, but for a box man it is a paltry sum not worth accepting. Generally people know too little about box men. They take too casually the meaning the box has for a box man. I'm not bluffing. With pure bluff alone, one can't go on living in a box for three years. They say that even in the case of the hermit crab, once it begins its life under its shell, the back part of the body, being covered by the carapace, becomes soft and thus breaks into pieces and the crab dies if forced out. A box man can't very well take off his box and simply return to the

ordinary world. When he takes it off it is to emerge into another world just as an insect metamorphoses. I secretly expected
that my meeting with her would provide that opportunity.

From the human chrysalis that is the box man,
    Even I know not
      What kind of living being will issue forth.

In a Mirror

The rain had turned to a light drizzle, but the wind had
risen. With every sigh of the breeze splashing drops flew
like the waving tentacles of a jellyfish. It was quite impossible
to see through. However, perhaps because of the placement
of the buildings, only the red gate light of the hospital at
the top of the slope that was my destination was always
and from everywhere visible. It was enveloped in dark green
and seemed like a stain in my eyes. I had taken the road any
number of times, but this was the first time I had walked
it wearing a box. Considering that, it seemed terribly far.
Usually when I was in the box, distance was seldom a serious
obstacle.

When anyone comes into contact with the scenery
around him, he tends to see selectively only those elements
necessary. For example, though one remembers a bus stop,
one can have absolutely no recollection of a large willow
tree nearby. One's attention is caught willy-nilly by the
hundred-yen piece dropped on the road, but the bent and
rusty nail and the weeds by the wayside may just as well not
be there. On the average road one usually manages not to
go astray. However, as soon as one looks out of the box's

observation window, things appear to be quite different. The various details of the scenery become homogeneous, have equal significance. Cigarette butts . . . the sticky secretion in a dog's eyes . . . the windows of a two-story house with the curtains waving . . . the creases in a flattened drum . . . rings biting into flabby fingers . . . railroad tracks leading into the distance . . . sacks of cement hardened because of moisture . . . dirt under the fingernails . . . loose manhole covers . . . but I am very fond of such scenery. The distance in it is fluid and the contours vague, and thus perhaps it resembles my own position. The scenery has the gentleness of a garbage dump. One never wearies of looking at such a view as long as one is peering out from a box.

But the effect of the box was reduced to nothing as I took the rising road to the hospital. The red light remained far off in the distance. A stain the color of blood deep within my closed eyes. The road was of gravel, and the space at my feet was not so dark as elsewhere. This scenery seemed to urge people to keep going, its details were all abridged. After that, a dimly white sky (clouds were beginning to cross from the west). Perhaps it was because the night was too dark (hence I abhor the night). It might also be, perhaps, that my destination was too well defined.

Despite all of that I shook my box and continued doggedly walking. But the box could not make time along the road. Since the ventilation was bad, I broke out in a sweat. Even the insides of my ears itched with the dampness. As I leaned forward, the box tilted, and there was the sound of it striking my hips. The very fragile sound of something made of paper.

Suddenly I heard the violent breathing of some beast. A huge growling mongrel brushed against my knees with its shoulder, and ran off at once. His wet back appeared to be dyed red. When I raised my head, I saw the red gate light.

The mist peeled away and a closed iron portal came into view. There was a special bell for night use painted with a phosphorescent color. I didn't want to ring the bell and have them open the door. Nor did I want to come face to face with the doctor. Stepping over the hedge, I entered the garden.

The dog had arrived before me and was waiting, but he made no pretense of barking. I had won him over by giving it some food beforehand. A light was burning faintly in one window. A luxuriant tangle of weeds twined around my feet. Apparently the remains of an old flower bed. I stumbled over the edging stones, and the dog, misunderstanding, frolicked around me. When I stood still and took a breath, sweat poured out and ran into my eyes.

Her room was in the back of the building, second window from the left. She had dropped the money to me less than an hour ago—possibly she was still awake. Even if she had dozed off, it would only be a light sleep. I need have no concern that she would set up a din on waking up surprised. I wanted to have a serious talk with her (even through the window, if that were possible) return the fifty thousand yen, and get her to cancel the promise I had made to throw the box away. Depending on her attitude, it was conceivable that I could assist her in another way.

But I wondered why there was a light in the window facing the garden. Over there was the waiting room, next, the examination room, and further inside that I assumed were the examination instruments. Twelve o'clock had come and gone, and I thought that one way or another they had forgotten to turn the light out, but for some reason I was uneasy. To be on the safe side, I decided to have a little look.

The window was rather high and the lower half was frosted glass. I could see only the ceiling. The light that came from below what seemed to be a floor lamp spread out diagonally in a parabola toward the inner part of the room. In order to see more, I needed something to stand on. It was out of the question to turn on a light and look around. Fortunately I remembered I had put the rear-view mirror from my car in my tote bag. I had had the feeling that it would come in handy and had stashed it away instead of tossing it out. After wiping off the dirt, I held it up diagonally and peered into it from below. Stretching my one arm and looking up through the space in the narrow window was laborious work. But my labors bore fruit. Contrary to my expectations (I had assumed that top and bottom would be reversed), I was able to view everything at an almost perfect angle.

The first thing I could see was an electric table lamp sitting on a corner of a big work desk. Then a large, whitish expanse. As I held the mirror stable, the white separated into walls and a door. Walls and door were old, and the several layers of paint could not conceal the scratches on the surface. The typically high hospital bed in the corner by the window was, of course, white too. The bookcase, crammed with old magazines and books, was painted white like the rest, but was somewhat less fresh. The room was simply spacious and without interest on the whole, though there was a stereo set beside the work desk; it was apparently the doctor's sitting room–study.

Indeed, the room itself was of little importance. When I put my recollections in order later, such was the arrangement. There were two people in it. I was completely fascinated by them. Other things were merely the reflections of mosaic fragments, compounded, as in the eye of some insect.

One was the girl, and since it was in the same building as her room, it was natural for her to be. there. She was stark naked. She was standing facing me stark naked in the middle of the room, and she was talking to someone about something.

The person who was being addressed was a box man. He was seated on the edge of the bed and was wearing a box exactly like mine. From where I was, only the back and the right side were visible; it was a cardboard box, exactly the same as my own—from the degree of dirtiness to the remains of the printed letters giving the name of a commercial product . . . to say nothing of the size. It was a fake replica of myself, imitated by design. And inside . . . the doctor, I presumed.

(Suddenly it occurred to me. Somewhere I remembered having seen exactly the same scene as this.)

Alone in the room with the naked girl . . . it was as if I could vividly feel her nakedness with my hands. But when . . . where? No, I must not be deceived, this was not a memory but a hallucination stemming from my desire. I could not believe that I had come visiting like this, that my objective was simply the repayment of the fifty thousand yen. Somewhere in my heart I must have secretly wished for this scene really to materialize. Yes, seeing her naked . . . stripping her naked body even more bare until I could see a nakedness beyond mere nudity.

> (Marginal note—red ink: Why do I persist in staring like this? Perhaps because I am too cowardly. Or perhaps because I am too curious. When I think about it, I fancy I have become a box man just to go on being a voyeur forever. I want to spy on all sorts of places, and the box is a portable hole that occurred to me under the circumstances, it being impossible to punch holes throughout the world. I also feel like running away and also like pursuing. Which is it to be?)

My desire to spy on the girl was clearly beginning to exceed the capacities of the box. I have the feeling that my mouth is packed full with distended and aching gums. But I alone am not to be blamed. She too had dropped an indirect hint. Aside from the fifty thousand yen paid by the doctor for the box, she suggested a special bonus from her to me as a photographer.

When my shoulder had been treated I tried patching together the story of her life, which she told me in bits and pieces: Until accepting her present position as apprentice nurse, she had been a poor art student (let's not ask whether she had any talent in these circumstances) and made a living by posing for those who belonged to privately run art schools or amateur art clubs. (She said it had left a bitter taste, resembling regret.) Two years ago she had had an abortion in this hospital (she was beginning to exist for me physically). Her convalescence was not satisfactory, and while she was in the hospital free of charge for about three months, a nurse who had been working there left, and the girl had taken her place for no particular reason (an aspect of her personality irked people and was hard to understand). She was busy with her work, but then she was assured of all her treatment in payment for it. As long as there was no special emergency, she had enough time to paint her pictures in the evenings and in her time off. But income aside, the modeling she had done before was apparently the work she liked best. It was not because she could take it easy, she insisted innocently. And while it wasn't especially pressured work, it had been tiring, and one needed stamina. She had said that the excitement of exposing her naked body as a model was the spice of life and inspired in her the will to create. (I considered that wrong. Incidentally, pictures of her are completely nonrepresentational and have no connection with any model.) She spoke as if she would still be doing modeling if the doctor had not strongly objected.

However much she was interested in my profession as a photographer, this was an obvious provocation. From the air-gun bullet that had come from the wound in my shoulder and from the way my hair was raggedly cut, she must have already guessed that I was a box man without his disguise. But I had overlooked her pretense. I had the feeling of licking her wound with the generosity of a protector. At such times a discharge came from my eyes. I braced myself, determined to break her with my own hands before she was broken by someone else. Teeth sprouted on my upper and lower eyelids. At the wild idea of nibbling at her, my eyeballs flushed hot and I got erections.

In a sense, this wild idea materialized. The naked girl . . . I who spied on her . . . I was indeed watching the naked her. But it was a conditional nakedness. It was a nakedness already looked upon by someone else, and that was the fake me. Far from being satisfied by seeing her naked, my jealousy increased because someone else had seen her. When one's throat becomes dry, it serves no purpose to be shown a picture of oneself drinking. At the same time as I was looking at her, another I was looking at me looking at her. I recalled a dream in which I had writhed desperately as I floated near the ceiling and looked down on my own dead body. I was ashamed and laughed scornfully at myself. The strength left my arm, the mirror tilted wildly, and the room flew off. I shifted it to my other hand and this time rested the edge of the mirror on the windowsill to keep it steady. When you're thirsty you can't help running in the direction of illusory water, even though you realize it's a mirage.

The two were facing each other separated by about four paces. Her attitude was relaxed, and to my regret I could not detect the slightest antagonism between them. I wondered if she had already reported on what had happened an hour ago. Supposing that the two were in league with each other, they would really be laughing at me. A foolishly honest box man who had only been waiting to be tossed fifty thousand yen like a reward to some dog, spending as he had promised a half day watching the whirlpools under the bridge . . . box head . . . toilet box . . . sheltered man in a box . . . box juggler.

But on the part of the naked girl I could feel not the slightest malice or machination. Though I experienced a sense of humiliation as before, no feelings of hatred welled up in me. I intently followed on her heels. My water jar that had been stolen by the fake box man. Her naked body was far more charming than I had imagined it to be. It was natural; there was no question of my imagination being able to catch up with her actual nakedness. Since this nakedness existed only while I was looking at it, my desire to see it became poignant too. Since it would vanish the minute I stopped looking, I should photograph it, or get it down on canvas. The naked body and the body are different. The naked body uses the actual physical body as its material and is a work of art kneaded by fingers which are the eyes. Although the physical body might be hers, concerning the proprietorship of the naked body, I had no intention of retreating in impotent envy.

Her naked body was supported by the left leg, as if it were floating lightly in water. It was as if a mysterious cord stretched straight from the tips of a magician's fingers. The toes of her right foot were placed over the instep of the left, and the bent knee opened slightly outward. What, I wondered, attracted me so much about that leg? Was it that it suggested the sexual organs? Judging from the cut of clothes today, perhaps one could consider the reproductive organs belonging to the legs rather than to the trunk. But if that were all, many other legs are more sexy. When one lives in

The last freight of that day had started out
from the sectional branch line to the main
line, listing far toward the outside and making
the switches creak. Absently watching the red
taillight, the trainman saw a cardboard box
fall to the tracks and tilted his head in perplexity.
The box began to walk.

a box, one looks principally at the lower half of people, and it's the legs one is familiar with. The femininity of legs, whatever you say, lies, I think, in the simple fluidity of the curving surfaces. The bones, tendons, and joints are completely fused in the flesh and have no effect on the surface. Certainly legs are much more suitable as covers for the sexual organs than as instruments for walking (I am not being sarcastic, there's no need for that; it is natural that a cover be needed for such a precious vessel). Eventually you've got to open the cover with your hands. Thus the charm of feminine legs (and he who denies that charm is a hypocrite) can only be tactile rather than visual.

However, I don't mean that her very visual legs are masculine. A man's legs, thanks to having continuously carried weight against the pull of gravity, are knotty, and the deeply imbedded joints spread horizontally; they are practical mechanisms for walking. But no matter how one searches, one can find absolutely no visible traces in her legs of the effort she expends to support her weight. To make a venturesome comparison, her legs are the pliant, fully extended legs of an adolescent before he has undergone a change of voice. Things that suddenly incite longing in a man exhausted from walking: for example, the lightness of a bird . . . the sensation of walking free from gravity. Willful legs that do not continually go against gravity like those of a man nor give up walking like those of a woman. A hasty retreat—the same as sex—is liable to provoke pursuit. Sexual attraction is not particularly lacking in her legs (even coverless sex is provocative enough). But even if I find my way to her sex, I feel that somehow there's something more to it. I wonder if I have discovered the ideal legs in hers or whether I am trying to fit her legs to the ideal.

White globular forms tilted diagonally. Compared with the legs, the buttocks as you might expect are tactile.

Perhaps it is because the center of gravity lies in the single deep crevasse. The raised right hipbone juts out, describing a smooth curve like that of a bird's breastbone. A faint smoke wells up from the crotch. Its tip, like a shadow, is subtly teased by the wind. But when I looked at the soft light hair on her head, and saw that it wasn't moving in the slightest, I realized that the wind was blowing only below. I assumed the fan was poorly regulated; and the cool air flowed along the floor. The hips had a tendency to draw back, and the stomach filling out generously gave the feeling of being terribly defenseless. The shoulders were bent far back, and the neck rising perpendicularly from there supported a head bent forward as if a hinge had come loose. It was an altogether relaxed pose, but I had the impression that a slender steel core passed down the middle of her. The right arm was positioned in the vicinity of the navel, the left near the solar plexus, and her position was such that she seemed to be embracing herself. Since her chest was stretched back, her breasts seemed smaller than they actually were. Under them were red marks left by the brassière. There was a line above the hipbone too, that was apparently left by her underwear. It would seem that not much time had gone by since she had taken them off and thrown them aside. The clothes she had removed lay in lumps at her feet. On the nurse's white uniform the tiny black undies stretched out like a dead spider.

She lightly bit her underlip. But spreading wide to both sides, it escaped from her teeth. Seeing her full-mouthed smile, I felt my heart cut by the blade of a faint sadness. Her raised eyes, filled with coquetry, looked up at the fake box. He apparently said something (obviously it was a random remark), and the girl raised her face and said two or three words in reply. The muscles of her back stretched like a steel measuring tape. She rose on tiptoes and began walking in the direction of the box. "You're going wrong!" I shouted involuntarily in my heart. My diaphragm stiffened, like wet leather, my breath shortened, and my face with lines of sweat spilling down from my hairline resembled the stripes on an overripe melon. She took something from the box. It was a glass with some beer still in it. I did not at all like her drinking from the same glass as the fake box man. All my muscles were ready to break through the windowpane and jump into the room, but because of her betrayal I knew I wouldn't do it (an example of a box man-like excuse). Some way or another she had drunk down about half of the beer with an awkward movement of the mouth as if she were sucking up spaghetti. She returned the glass to the box, and, swinging her body, she took several great steps backward. I was relieved when I realized that the fake box man had not left his box. The tension that reached from my shoulders to my hips relaxed, and I made a noise like the tearing away of something pasted. She returned to her former position and was saying something rapidly. Suddenly she shut her mouth, looked up at the ceiling, and began to pass her two hands over her hips. Again the box man took over the initiative of the conversation, which she apparently didn't find very interesting.

Abruptly pivoting on her heels, she turned her back. Then all at once she dropped to all fours on the floor, placing her elbows and knees together and assuming a posture in which her hips jutted up higher than the rest of her. The direct light that did not pass through the shade of the lamp made her seem exaggeratedly tactile and globular. Her breasts were a lid on the inside of the inverted triangle formed by her trunk, thighs, and upper arms. My whole body began to wither away, leaving only my eyes. The fake box man, bending forward, swayed slowly back and forth.

Suddenly the ground at my feet surged up as if it had been kneaded, and, losing my balance, I sank to one knee.

I still had enough wits not to make any noise. But it wasn't the surface of the ground that was heaving; the dog, bored, had squeezed himself in between my knees. It was difficult to chase it away quietly. I couldn't make any noise, and I couldn't let him bark. But he continued to grow more and more excited, and with all his strength, he thrust his nose like a piece of wet soap between my legs. It evidently intended to get into the box with me. Having little choice, I punctured a small hole in a can of beef and after letting him sniff the gravy and lick it, I flung the can as far away as I could. I knew the poor thing would be wrestling with the can until tomorrow morning.

I hurried back to the window. The surface of the mirror was smudged with my fingers. I hastily wiped it with my shirttail and set it up again. The scene had changed completely. Fortunately what I had been so apprehensive about had not taken place at all. The fake box, neither torn up nor broken to bits, was still sitting in the same position on the edge of the bed. Of course, even wearing the box, he might have been able to take advantage of her. If he had bored a hole for his penis and was prepared for some unnatural positions, it would have been possible. But to do that he would need her cooperation, and that would take a good deal of time. Had it taken me that long to chase the dog away? I wondered. Perhaps it had, but anyway she was no longer naked. She was smoking a cigarette, leaning against the work desk in the corner of the room. Even the buttons of the too-long white uniform were carefully buttoned, and her legs could no longer be seen. With her legs invisible, she seemed strangely distant, another person. About a third of the cigarette was consumed. Tired, forbidding eyebrows. An enema syringe peeked out from the pocket of her white uniform. Her slender sinewy fingers were encircled by the rubber tube of the syringe, and her fingernails bore a silver polish. It was unbelievable that she had been naked a few minutes before. Or was it that everything had been merely a mirage in the mirror?

From somewhere beyond the shrubbery came the sad breathing of the dog pounding against the ground with the can gripped in his teeth. When I rubbed my neck, lumps of dirt kept coming off. And as I gathered them into patties, I was terribly depressed. I seemed to be somehow profoundly hurt by what in fact had not happened—the scene in which she was violated by the box—something I didn't want to happen, something that absolutely couldn't have happened. Perhaps it was because I have all too often been outwitted.

Rubbing out her cigarette, she nodded her head, scratching inside her ear with the little finger of her free hand. When the light from the lamp struck her straight on, the space between her two eyes opened up, and she appeared slightly walleyed. She laughed only with her mouth, showing her teeth suspiciously, whereupon her face turned into that of an obstinate child. When she closed her mouth, shaking her head slightly to the right and left, the lower projecting lip was unexpectedly voluptuous. Then slightly shifting the upper part of her body, she adopted the stance of kicking an invisible paper balloon. She crossed the room toward the door. When she began to walk, I saw that it was indeed her. There was a giddy lightness to her body. And I wondered if this most familiar sense of weightlessness was a sense of falling. The fake box man crawled down from the bed. Without even looking back, she pulled the door knob, and swinging around the door, disappeared on the other side. The box man who tried to chase her resembled an insect whose limbs had been torn off. Except for the fact that he was not wearing rubber boots, he was my mirror image, even to the canvas around his waist. The door closed, and the box man came to a halt. Evidently he did not want to pursue her too far. Shaking the box, he changed directions and came shuffling back as if his underclothes were wet. I could see the front of the box. The hanging vinyl was exactly the same color and arrangement as my own (other than that there was not a single little hole in the box—not even a penis hole).

Nevertheless, it was an elaborate reproduction. It was overly elaborate for ordinary purposes. What was he hatching up? Judging from the present state of affairs, no matter how determined I was to return the fifty thousand yen, it looked as if it wasn't going to be very easy to get him to agree to it. From the instant I took the money, the right of being a real box man had shifted to the other party, and perhaps it was I who had become the fake. My shadow came and went with the tottering steps of a toy robot following the diagonal across the room. It was not very pleasant to see my image in the mirror, ignoring my will, moving around as it wished. Stupid man! Why didn't he take the box off right away? Perhaps he was drunk. If he continued like that, he wouldn't be able to get out of the box at all. Well, if he didn't want to leave it, that was just fine too. If he wanted, I could just as well get out of my box instead of him. I felt that leaving the box was a possible course of action. Perhaps, if I dare engage in wishful thinking, her original objective in dreaming up this deal was to confine him to the box. Then she would be free. How would it be if I used this as an opportunity to sever all connection with my box?

I decided for the time being to leave. There was no merit in simply hastening the conclusion. If I just made up my mind, I could remove the box at any point. After taking my time and getting my feelings in order, it might be just as well to come again tomorrow. Before leaving, I decided to have a peep into her room. I crossed over the gravel path that led to the entrance (being covered with dirt, it made no noise). Turning the box sideways, I pushed my way into the thicket of asters as tall as a man. A cleavage like the inside of a convoluted shell flickered in my eyes—perhaps it was due to some association of ideas that came from the intense fragrance of the grass. Perhaps it was the hollow under her armpits. But the back of the building faced northward, and all the windows were small and high. Her windows especially were cut off by heavy curtains and I could barely distinguish any light, but I had not hoped for anything more. Not yet ready to give up, I kept waiting for something, concealed under the eaves. The wind shook the gutter, making great drops fall down, and my box resounded like a bass drum. But there was no reaction from her room.

Of course, it was nothing at all to get out of the box. And since there was nothing to it, I felt no compulsive need to leave it. Yet I wanted someone, if possible, to lend me a hand.

Three-and-a-Half-Page Insert on Different Paper

(It's not only the paper that's dissimilar. For the first time a fountain pen is being used, and the writing is clearly different. If in time someone makes a clear copy in a new notebook with other notes, they should simply standardize the paper and the writing. There's no need to worry about the difference in writing and in paper now.)

—Well then. Now what? (said the doctor).
—I'm thirsty. (she complained).

—There's a crack in that glass.

—I don't care.

—Well . . . ?

—I took them off . . . just as I promised.

—I'm asking about the light.

—Is this all the beer there is?

—I'm interested in how dark it was as you were taking your clothes off.

—It was pitch black. It was so dark it took me a long time to unfasten my brassière.

—There's no relationship between the light and the brassière. Anyway you can do that by touch.

—Well, I suppose so, but . . .

—Let it go. And then what?

—He lost patience and insisted on helping me unfasten the brassière . . . he wouldn't listen.

—Strange.

—Why?

—It was pitch black, wasn't it? How did he know you were having trouble with the brassière?

—Oh, he just knew . . . some way or other.

—Then you did get him to help?

—Not at all.

—Why?

—I made a promise, didn't I, absolutely not to let him touch me? Besides, see how long my arms are. I can shake hands behind my back.

—All right. So then you took off your clothes in the dark, and after you had finished, you turned on the light. Is that right?

—Yes, I think so. . . .

—Well, what about the shot?

—I gave it, of course.

—Naked?

—You can't break the capsule by feel.

—Being naked's enough. It's ridiculous to go so far as giving a shot naked.

—It comes to the same thing, doesn't it?

—There's a big difference.

—Don't raise your voice so.

—Listen to me. You're a lot more frankly naked when some of your clothes are off than when they're all off. The same logic holds true for shots. A naked body doing something is more completely naked than a simple nude. You can't get away with saying you didn't know it.

—I realize that. I'll be careful from now on.

—Try repeating what happened in order once more from the beginning.

—So I took off my clothes, turned on the light . . .

—Before that, the light was out, wasn't it?

—So I turned out the light, took off my clothes, turned on the light, and then gave the shot.

—Pretty amazing. During all that time you didn't say a word . . . isn't it?

—I don't mean that . . .

—We're going to be in trouble if you abridge whenever you want.

—He didn't say anything important. It's true. I recall we talked about the weather . . . as he patted my hair like this . . .

—You promised not to let him use his hands.

—But it was only my hair.

—It's the same thing . . . anywhere . . .

—But he just happened to touch my hair just by chance, and . . .

—Don't shield him.

—It was just when I was leaning over to turn on the lamp by the pillow.

—The lamp?

—He asked me to.

—What?

—There are places you can't see very well with the light coming only from above.

—Drop it there. There'll be no end to it if you spoil him so much.

—You're right. I'll be careful.

—Then what did he say?

—He said it looked like rain . . . since my hair was winding into little curls.

—You were just wet with perspiration.

—Yes, I was dripping.

—But just a minute. Before his weather report, you were asked to put the light on, weren't you?

—Yes, the light came first.

—You're not reliable.

—I'm sorry. I'm already exhausted. I'm not suited to this sort of thing. Look, my legs are trembling as if I'd got on top of an electric washer.

—Well, come over here. My lap's better than any washer.

—I'd like a smoke.

—Smoking late at night makes your skin rough.

—It's better than being naked.

—You're exaggerating. Don't go thinking a fellow like that's a man. Being naked in front of him is no more than taking your panties off in the bathroom.

—You, Doctor, are the one who's concerned with my nakedness in front of him. You ask too many questions.

—I only want to know the truth.

—I'd at least like to forget what's over.

—Apparently there are things you want to forget at any cost.

—Unfortunately they're nothing you imagine, Doctor.

—If that's true, fine.

—It is. First he wiped away the eye mucus and made me take all kinds of poses; he watched me as if he were on a treasure hunt. But the shot began to take effect at once, and the look in his eyes gradually became strange. In less than five minutes he was staring at the fluorescent light and seemed quite oblivious of me.

—It's all right to let him dream the way he wants.

—But last of all he made me give him an enema.

—An enema?

—It was too much. The same question over and over. I wondered if he would never tire of asking. Imagine it . . . he asked me to check to see whether he had an erection or not. I was so annoyed I fooled him and told him it looked about eighty percent up. Immediately he got angry. He told me to stop talking nonsense, that he should know best about himself.

—If he knew, he didn't have to ask you, did he?

—Then he began badgering me. When he smelled my perspiration he apparently got an erection, so he told me to get more to the side.

—Don't joke. What part of the castrated pig was up, I wonder.

—Well, he wasn't up. He began to cry instead. I was amazed. Or maybe he was pretending to cry. When I looked closely I could see he was crying, but only by the set of his mouth and his voice. And then . . . what halitosis! As long as he was badgering me, I could stand it only by holding my breath. He was apparently rather excited. He said he couldn't stand looking up my crotch when I was on all fours.

—Did you go so far as to do that?

—Not at all. It was the fault of the shot. I just stood there stock still. And he just imagined what he wanted. But it's strange, isn't it. Maybe that's hypnotism. He wasn't actually seeing me, yet just by thinking that he wanted to, I somehow came to have the impression I was being seen. From the moment I thought I was being seen by him all my strength suddenly left me, and I was unable to give up imagining I was on all fours. The blood left my buttocks, and they grew pale and numb. I had the feeling of turning into a stone.

—What about the enema, then?

—Oh, that was later. Suddenly just when he stopped crying, he let out a scream like a patient with a heart attack, saying to hurry up, that he wanted nitroglycerine.

—A weird fellow.

—All the same, he didn't have an erection, but apparently there was some reaction. He ground his teeth and panted, and when I listened closely I could hear him saying, "Thanks . . . thanks."

—Why didn't you refuse the enema?

—You yourself said not to take it seriously, didn't you?

—Quite true, quite true.

—Please, let me rest. I wanted you to tell me that all this was unimportant.

—Well, let's take a pause here. Don't just stand there . . . come over here. Take off your stockings.

—I'm not wearing any stockings.

—Hurry up, come on. . . . What sort of pose did he explicitly want you to take?

—Turn off the light. . . .

In Which It Is a Question of the Sullen Relationship Between the I Who Am Writing and the I Who Am Being Written About

The naked girl on all fours. The inverted triangle formed by her torso, her thighs, and her upper arms was burned deep into the backs of my eyeballs; and wherever I looked a flesh-colored openwork forever overlaid my field of vision. The pores of my whole body opened their mouths at the same time, and tongues dangled limply from them. I was nauseous . . . abnormally tense . . . from lack of air. I had not had enough sleep either.

Nonetheless, when and how did I get to this point? Apparently I'm deceiving myself. Eighteen minutes past three. Now I'm here at the municipal seaside bathhouse facing the Port of T across the harbor. A deserted sandy beach where hermit crabs crawl noisily about. A soaked green triangular flag flapping round a bamboo pole. No matter how much of the way back here is downhill, I couldn't possibly have just come rolling down. I must have had some purpose, whatever it was.

As a matter of fact, it was right here that I had made my preparations a week before to go to the hospital to get treatment for my wound. It's an ideal place for a box man to leave his box unnoticed. I wanted to clean my underwear and my shirt, shave, and wash my hair, to say nothing of my body. I was free to use the hydrant at the station or the boat landing, but the crowds came here late, and if I choose my time well I can take it easy and use the shower in the dressing room without being questioned by anyone.

I really don't have to hide. Just a moment ago, I finished doing what I had come for. I had cleaned my underwear, shaved my beard, washed my hair and my body. To avoid catching a cold I withdrew temporarily to the box until my underwear and shirt were dry, but this was purely to tide me over, and I intended to leave it presently. Yes, I had the impression of being already half out. You don't need any particular resolution to scratch where you're bitten by an insect. The exit to the tunnel was visible right there. If the box is a moving tunnel, the naked girl is a dazzling light flowing in the entrance, waiting intently to be seen. I think that surely here is the opportunity I have been waiting for for three years.

Furthermore, I unexpectedly met the fake box man. My replica was fixedly staring at the girl on all fours with her rump high in the air (defenselessly waiting to be seen). So far I had not felt that the box was all that unsightly. What was disagreeable was the recurrent dream where I became a ghost, and hovering at the ceiling, looked down on my own dead body. Could I still have a lingering attachment for the box at this point? Far from that, I was already thoroughly bored with it. A tunnel is functional only because it has an exit. It makes absolutely no difference if I tear these notes up and throw them away as soon as I finish this last line here. . . .

It can't be very long since I began living in a box. I once saw a broken and empty cardboard box roughly stuffed

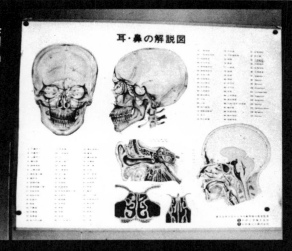

病室禁煙

耳・鼻の解説図

I am now looking around the inside of the box . . . a cube slightly more spacious than my own capacity . . . cardboard walls tanned by sweat and sighs . . . graffiti inscribed with a ballpoint pen all over in small letters . . . reverse tatooing . . . a not very prepossessing personal filigrain . . .

into the narrow space between a public john and a board fence (perhaps around some outdoor parking lot). The box with its resident gone was like a deserted house. The aging process had apparently been rapid, and the box had weathered to the color of withered grapes. But at a glance I was able to distinguish that it was the discarded skin of a box man. There, where it appeared half torn away, was what remained of the observation window . . . the curled vinyl curtain was still pasted on. On the sides the protuberant clusters of little holes for hearing were all swollen like some skin disease. I tried to strip away the surface. It sounded like adhesive plaster tearing off, and the inside of the box was visible. I instinctively inserted myself into the space and concealed this sloughed-off skin from the gaze of those passing by.

On the inside of the box, like a handprint impressed in clay, the traces of the life of the former occupant (let us give him the name B for the moment) were vividly and negatively etched. There were the traces of the cheap chopsticks he had used to strengthen the torn places by attaching them with insulation tape, and clippings of nude photos, now faded and bearing stains the color of bird droppings. There was a red cord to tie to the trouser belt so that the box would not shake; a little plastic box was located underneath the observation window. Further, traces of numerous graffiti covered the entire surface. Large and small white rectangular spaces outlined the spots where such things as the radio, the bag, and the flashlight had formerly been suspended.

My strength drained away and I felt cold. I had the feeling of witnessing the opening of the sarcophagus of B's mummy. I quivered. I had never contemplated my own (my box's) death in such a form. I intended to vanish naturally—when the time came—like a volatilized drop of water. But this was the real world, not imagination. How in heaven's name had B met his end?

Of course, it did not necessarily follow that the death of the box was exactly B's physical death. Perhaps he just passed through the tunnel and threw the box away. The corpse of the box became a butterfly (if a butterfly is too romantic, then a cicada will do, or a May fly), the cast-off skin of a chrysalis that has flown away. I wanted to think it was possible. If I didn't, I couldn't have been able to stand it. And to do so I needed proof. I concentrated my gaze on the graffiti all around, searching for evidence. Unfortunately B apparently regularly used a felt-tip marker, the ink of which was water soluble, and deciphering was nigh impossible. There was a cover on the little plastic box. If there was some clue it would surely be in there. When I wrenched off the incrusted top the hinge split open. Inside were two ball-point pens, a handleless knife, a flint for a lighter, a crystal-less watch with only the minute hand, and then a small notebook with the cover missing. The first page of the note-book began in this way. Fortunately I copied it on the spot on the inner side of my box (at the time there was still a lot of blank space left), and I am able to quote it exactly.

> *"His concern was excessive. When he was absent from his room even a little longer than usual, he worried lest in the meantime the room might not have disappeared, and he could not go out in peace. Gradually his proclivity to stay at home grew worse. It got to the point where he would shut himself up in his room, unable to take a step outside. In the end he died either from hunger or by hanging. Of course, I hear that no one has as yet identified the corpse."*

When I tried turning the next page the notebook fell apart between my fingers like a soaked biscuit. With it my evidence crumbled away too, and I was still unable to assess the significance of the crushed and empty box-corpse.

Now should I bid goodbye to the box? But my underwear and my shirt for some reason were taking a long time to dry. The rain had lifted, but because of the moisture-laden, low clouds they were long in drying. Fortunately I felt fine there naked in the box. Perhaps it was because I had carefully cleaned off the dirt, but the various parts of my body felt strangely fresh, and I even experienced an actual longing to embrace myself. But I did not intend to stay like this for-ever. I hoped the morning calm would end soon.

The dark, wet sky and the black sea fused at eye level. The water was much darker than the sky. A deep black like an elevator falling. A bottomless black that you could still see even if you shut your eyes. I could hear the sea. I could see the inside of my own cranium. A dome-shaped tent whose inner struts are exposed. Exactly like the inside of a dirigible. My complete lack of sleep sends my blood pound-ing. I wanted to sleep. I wanted to sleep at least two or three hours before leaving the box. I tried shutting my eyes even tighter than they were. Waves became visible. Waves in regularly receding, gradually narrowing parallel lines kept rolling ceaselessly toward the open sea. There were a front and back to the successive waves, and the front part glinted slightly. As I leaned forward, trying to see through them, my right and left eyeballs popped out and dropped straight down. And from where they had fallen a wisp of smoke came wafting up. As the eyeballs bounced against each other, they kept rolling between the waves. I felt nauseous. I opened my eyes. Sea and sky stood still, blackly, and everything was as it had been originally. I was miserably small on the hard, wet sand. Apparently I could only wait with my eyes open until I was overcome with sudden sleep.

But even if I can't catch a nap, I must, under any circumstances, begin the planned course of action when the time comes. After disposing of the box that I have taken off, I shall visit the hospital again at precisely eight o'clock. Since outpatients start coming at ten, I shall anticipate as much extra time as possible before that. However, if I am too early, I will incur their displeasure and that will cause problems. Eight o'clock is a good time, and I won't disturb them while they are still asleep. I estimate that I can get them to spare me a couple of hours for negotiations, though I can't go so far as to say that that will be sufficient. It's possible that I could get them to take the day off from examinations and to make them accept going on with the negotiations. At any rate the negotiations will take plenty of time . . . but what negotiations . . . ?

> (Let me put this down before I forget. A clincher has just occurred to me that I should like to use when I see her. "I don't want you to laugh or get angry. I don't care about others laughing or getting angry, you're the one who's important.")

Now calm down. Let's go for broke. If I manage without a breakdown in the negotiations, I imagine they'll come to an agreement, and if they don't there's nothing to do but break off the negotiations. Rather than worrying about the negotiations, what is important now is to calculate the procedure necessary to arrange things so that I can be there at eight o'clock. I say arrange things, but there is nothing particularly troublesome. If I tear the box up into three or four pieces and fold them up, it will be ordinary trash. That will take scarcely five minutes at the most. Even if I liquidate my possessions, in any case they are articles of daily use for a life on the move, and they won't amount to much. For example, this plastic board that I am using now as a pad for my notes. It's simply a piece of rather thickish board, ordinary, milky white, sixteen by eighteen inches, but it is an absolutely essential item that I cannot do without in my life. First of all, it replaces a table. A stable level surface is necessary at all costs for eating and telling fortunes with cards. It also becomes a chopping board when I cook. It's a shutter against the rain over the observation window on winter nights when the wind is strong, and on summer evenings when there's no breeze at all it conveniently takes the place of a fan. It's a portable bench for sitting on the wet ground, and it becomes a perfect worktable for undoing the cigarette butts that I have collected and for rolling them again.

Of course, as it is, it has taken time and trouble to cull out my personal possessions as much as I have. When I first started living in a box, there was a time when I was quite unable to abandon the common idea of convenience and stored away willy-nilly things I didn't even know how to use, not to mention those articles that seemed as if they might come in handy. My baggage was endlessly increased with various items: a tin can on which were embossed three Technicolor nudes holding a golden apple (surely that would serve some purpose), a precious stone (perhaps an ancient implement), a slot-machine ball (it would come in handy for moving heavy things), a *Concise English-Japanese Dictionary* (indispensable sometime, one never knew), a high heel, painted gold (the shape was interesting, and it might be used in place of a hammer), a one-hundred-and-twenty-five-watt, six-ampere house socket (it would be a problem if it wasn't around when I needed it), a brass doorknob (attached to a string, that could be a dangerous weapon), a soldering iron (surely useful for something), a key ring with five keys (it was not impossible that sometime in the future I would come on a lock one of them would fit), a cast-iron nut one and five-eighths inches in diameter (suspended from a string, it could be a seismograph and would also be handy as a weight when I dried film). When it got so that I couldn't move for the cramped quarters and the weight, I was at last vividly aware of the necessity of throwing them all out. What a box man needs is obviously not a seven-appliance, all-purpose knife but some device that uses a single safety-razor blade for any number of purposes. If the article is not used at least three times a day, it should be disposed of with no regrets.

But there's a limit to throwing things away. It takes work to store articles too, but the effort required to throw them away is still greater. If one does not somehow hold one's possessions down, one is on tenterhooks lest they be blown away by the wind. For example, could a person who habitually used a small radio—a portable FM with quite good sound—dismiss it as trash just because he wanted to make his burden lighter? I, however, was able to do even that.

Indeed, I would certainly tell her about the radio. If the necessity arose, I should like to tell the fake box man too. Before the negotiations, I would like those two to understand clearly what sort of opponent they are dealing with.

—You're wondering what I have come for so early in the morning. (I address myself exclusively to her; as for the doctor, let him stay in the corner of the room with the fake box over his head just as he is.) I'm taking a simple stroll. A morning walk. It would be hard to draw the road up the slope from the soy-sauce factory, it's so dispersed, but I like it. What's the name of that ancient tree with the profusion of small leaves on the way? When the triangular hospital roof here came into view beyond the tree leaves, I became strangely nervous. It's an atmosphere where strange machinations are going on, with the small, high, painted windows in the cracked mortar wall. Don't you believe me? Then let me put it this way: there is no particular reason, I came just because I wanted to. You still don't believe me? Do I look as if I want that much? I was born with this face, and there's nothing I can do about it. It's a real handicap to have a face with shifty eyes. But look here, these fifty thousand yen . . . (saying this, I throw them onto the examination table . . . not too hard, but just hard enough). I took them for the time being, but I have not yet decided to accept them. Right now I'm seriously thinking about it. But don't worry, I disposed of the box as you ordered. So we're even . . . no, I'm the one who's owed something. How about it . . . how does it feel living in a box? (As I say this, I suddenly look in the window of the fake box, and without giving him time to answer, I immediately again turn toward the girl.) Now I'll get right to the point: I'd like for you to listen to a story about a radio so you can know what sort of person I am. Yes, a radio. Actually I was terribly addicted to news for a long time. I wonder if you see what I mean. I couldn't stand it if there weren't fresh news reports coming in one after the other all the time. Battlefield situations go on changing minute by minute. Moving picture stars and singers keep marrying and divorcing. Rockets go shooting off to Mars, and a fishing boat sends off an SOS and blacks out. A pyromaniacal fire chief is apprehended. When a venomous serpent escapes from a load of bananas and an employee of the Ministry of International Trade and Industry commits suicide and a little girl of three is raped, an international conference achieves great success and ends by collapsing, a society is formed to breed sterilized mice, a child is discovered buried in cement at the construction site of a supermarket, the total number of deserters from troops throughout the world sets a new record, the world seems to be boiling over like a teakettle. The globe's capable of changing shape the minute you take your eyes off it for even a second. I took seven different news-papers; I set up in my room two television sets and three radios; when I went out I never let a portable radio out of my hand, and when I went to sleep I left the earphones plugged in. I got different news reports on different stations at the same time, and there could be special news broadcasts at any moment. Timid animals keep too close a watch around them, and gradually like the giraffe their necks stretch or like the monkey they become incapable of coming down out of the trees. Don't laugh. For the one afflicted it's serious. He spends the greater part of the day just reading and listening to news. Angry with the weakness of his own will, still with aching heart, he is unable to separate himself from the radio or television. Of course, I was very much aware that no mat-ter how much I went rooting around for news I wouldn't necessarily come closer to the truth. I realized that, but I couldn't stop. Perhaps I needed the news form, which is summarized in clichés, not truth or experience. In short, I was thoroughly addicted to news.

One day, however, I suddenly recovered. A trivial event, served as an antidote, so really trivial that I myself inclined my head in disbelief. It was—where was it indeed?—oh, yes, at one corner of the wide sidewalk between the subway sta-tion and the bank. During the day few people pass that way. A middle-aged fellow who at first glance seemed to be a white-collar worker was walking in the most ordinary way right in front of me. Suddenly all the strength left his legs, and he moved as if to sit down, but fell on his side, and lay motionless. I had the feeling he was playing a game of big bad wolf with a child and had been shot. A young fellow with the air of a student, who was passing by, looked at the fallen man amused. "My God, he's dead!" he said. I remem-ber that he looked up at me shocked with a wan smile on his lips. I paid no attention, but he reluctantly went to use the telephone at a tobacconist's two or three stores farther on. Being a professional photographer—well, I was, merely to the extent of getting a job once or twice a month making commercial samples of insert advertisements—I at once set up my camera and tried focusing it from all sorts of angles. In the end I changed my mind and did not take a picture, but that was not because I was especially grieving over the corpse. It was because I realized at once that it would absolutely never become news.

Dying is, of course, a kind of transformation. First of all, the skin suddenly pales. Then the nose thins, and the jaw withers and gets smaller. The half-open mouth resembles the edge of a tangerine skin cut open with a knife, and the red artificial teeth of the lower jaw begin to jut out from the opening. Further, even the clothes that are being worn change. What appeared to be of very high quality turns before one's eyes into cheap goods, showy but worthless. Of course, such things are not news. But it would seem that for the dead man in question whether it's news or not has nothing to do with him. Supposing one is the tenth victim that had fallen into the hands of a much-wanted, fiendish killer, I don't suppose he would devise a particularly different way of dying. The dead person has changed himself, but the outside world has changed too, and things cannot change any more than they have. It's such a great change that no news, however big, can match it.

No sooner had I realized this than my thinking about news suddenly changed completely. How shall I say . . . ? Slogans won't do the trick: "You too can stop news-watching." But I think you understand . . . somehow . . . why everybody wants news the way they do. Are they preparing for times of emergency by knowing in advance the changes taking place in the world, I wonder? I used to think so. But that was a big lie. People listen to news only to feel reassured.

Because however great the news of catastrophe they hear, those listening are still perfectly alive. The really big news is the ultimate news announcing the end of the world, I suppose. Of course, everybody wants to hear that. For then one does not need to abandon the world alone. When I think about it, I feel the reason that I was addicted was my eagerness not to miss this ultimate broadcast. But as long as the news goes on, it will never get to the end. Thus news constitutes the announcement that it is still not the end of the world. The following trifling clichés are merely abridgments. Last night the greatest bombings of North Vietnam this year were carried out by B52s, but somehow you are still alive. Gas lines under construction ignited and eight persons received serious and light wounds, but you are alive and safe. Record rate of rising prices, yet you continue to live. Extinction of marine life in bays by waste products from factories, but somehow you survive everything.

—Now what were we talking about?

"You were saying, it seems to me, that you were bored listening to news," she said, rearranging her legs (apparently she was quite aware of where my interest lay) and lighting another cigarette that she had put to her lips.

From her side the fake box man added, in a muffled voice, "I don't understand at all. What's the use of introducing yourself the way you're doing?"

—What I'm saying is that there aren't any baddies among those who don't listen to news. (I rejected the doctor's words highhandedly and did not break my smile in the girl's direction.) I have no intention of changing things here arbitrarily, for not believing the news is, I think, not believing in change.

"Nevertheless, isn't it illogical?" interrupted the fake box man in an unexpectedly abrupt tone.

"What's illogical?" I said.

"I mean the fifty thousand yen. You took the money provisionally to buy a box, because I thought you were on intimate terms with the box man. It would indeed be illogical if you thought you could keep it or not."

"Stop twisting things," I said, flinching from the unexpected counterattack. "You already know very well that I'm identical to a box man."

"No, I don't. . . ."

"There's no use lying. I've proof." I inhaled slowly in order to calm down and then exhaled. "That morning about a week ago when I came to get my wound treated, you already saw very clearly that I was a real box man. My poorly trimmed hair . . . my sandpaper face covered with razor scars . . . although I smelled strongly of soap, bits of skin like dandruff continually peeled off on my neck and shoulders."

"But they say there are a lot of eccentrics among photographers, don't they?" she observed lightly as if pointing out a blunder in a game. Could it be that in the last analysis she was in league with the doctor and had simply taken advantage of me?

"But at the time—you admitted it yourself—it was an air-rifle bullet that was stuck in the wound in my shoulder."

"A lot of people around here have air rifles. Weasels apparently have easy pickings in the chicken houses."

"When I was hit, a thoughtful witness who happened to be present told me about this place. She even gave me the price of the medical treatment. Three thousand yen, in bills that smelled a bit of disinfectant," I said, staring deep into her eyes. I could not believe that she would betray me so easily. Hadn't she clearly promised to be my model? She said that when she modeled and felt the eyes of an artist on her she became supercharged. She had indeed been provocative then, but now she was temporizing in front of the doctor. It would be anything but desirable here to have the doctor get up on his high horse. By pushing her too far it was conceivable that I would worsen her position. "Some girl in a miniskirt riding on a new-style bicycle . . . perhaps it was a girl. Unfortunately I only saw her retreating figure, but the legs were terribly beautiful. They were legs that once seen were unforgettable. When you go on living in a box for a long time, since you naturally see only the lower half of those going by, your eyes become trained to see legs and only legs."

I had the feeling that her cheeks filled slightly with a certain smile. But it was the fake box man who laughed.

"Surely there's a big difference between wearing a box and looking at one."

"Let me remind you that I haven't yet completely renounced my rights of ownership."

"Indeed. There's a big difference," the fake box man repeated reflectively in a calm voice. "Last night for the first time I spent the whole night in the box. I understood the difference very well. No wonder one is ready to become a box man."

"I have no intention of holding you back by force."

"It's quite natural that you shouldn't."

A chuckle infected the fake box man's happy-go-lucky voice. It was both friendly and sarcastic, and I did not like it. It was as if it was out of tune. I felt rather that from the beginning I should have treated him as a fellow box man. Surely there was nothing at all to get excited about. If I were to broach the subject of advice for a box man after he goes out into town, such as methods of procuring foodstuffs, little-known but good places to find slightly used articles in relatively good shape, ways of obtaining long-distance free travel, or the whereabouts of at least seven fierce dogs to avoid within the city, then we should talk this thing over more calmly. But being in his presence was uncomfortable. Even though I realized that he was a copy of myself, I was embarrassed and shrank from doing so. In a situation like this perhaps I should have challenged him with my own box on. I shifted my attack to her.

"If it were up to you, what would you do? Would you keep him in check or would you let him do as he wished?"

She looked up at me, leaning lightly as she was against the corner of the examination table. As the corners of her mouth were drawn up, she seemed to be smiling, but her eyes did not smile at all.

"I simply think that if we suddenly gave out a tab indicating there was no examination, the patients would be inconvenienced."

That would be quite true. A sly answer that might be interpreted in a number of ways. But for the time being I suppose I should be content with that much. Now I only had to wait for the fake box man to make a statement.

The box, making a sound, drew my attention and leaned over as if to show off. The vinyl over the window separated and an eye looked out. An eye that simply looked, expressionless. An insolent eye that forced on me the role of being seen, but of not seeing. I wonder when he learned such a technique. It goes without saying that the model was myself. I was depressed. I was being seen, but was the one seeing too.

"No matter how much we exchange words, it's useless," said the fake box man in a small voice that was ill-suited to his appearance. "Anyway you wouldn't believe it."

"What?"

"You won't believe that I am going to leave here instead of you. In your heart you want that to happen, but you won't believe that I will."

"But you have no intention, actually, of leaving."

"I've prepared a little compromise plan." Clearing his throat, he continued in a lower, more obsequious tone. "For example, how would it be if we tried it this way? What about you making yourself at home in this house? No matter what relationship you establish with her I will absolutely not interfere. I will not interfere or meddle with you or cause you any trouble. But I want you to accept just one condition. I want you to give me the freedom of watching you. Just watching. Of course, wearing the box the way I am. Exactly the relationship that stands between the three of us now. I'm just asking you to let me watch from a corner like this. When you get used to me, I'll be just like a wastebasket."

Somehow I had the impression that I had had the fake box act in my place and made a proposition that I myself had formulated. When I stealthily stole a glance at the girl, she had begun concentrating on a stringless cat's cradle, rapidly moving the fingers of both hands. Slowly she shifted her legs. The hem of her pressed white uniform separated and knees peeped out and made me feel as if I should like to touch them with a finger on which saliva had been applied. Perhaps she was naked under the white dress. The rubber balloon I had swallowed, that had some device for making it swell and which I knew nothing about, I suddenly felt expand in my stomach. Nevertheless, I wondered if I would have the courage in front of the fake box man to ask her to strip off her clothes.

"There's nothing to hesitate about," continued the fake box man encouragingly. "If you pay no attention to a box man, he's just like wind or dust. I myself had an interesting experience in this respect. When I developed a photo I had casually taken, right there in the picture was a close-up of something quite unexpected. A man with a cardboard box over his head was nonchalantly walking by. Since I'm no expert like you, the camera was anything but sophisticated.

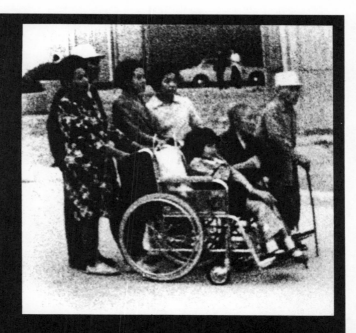

In seeing there is love, in being seen there is abhorrence. One grins, trying to bear the pain of being seen. But not just anyone can be someone who only looks. If the one who is looked at looks back, then the person who was looking becomes the one who is looked at.

I wonder just what I intended to take a picture of. This happened some time ago, but I think it was the scene of some funeral. I had decided to take pictures of the funeral of a patient that I had treated myself . . . as remembrances. Even so, I was surprised. I should have seen him with my own eyes since he was so close. Yet I have absolutely no recollection. If a ghost is something that is not visible, yet which one has the impression of being able to see, a box man is just the opposite. It was since then that I began to be interested in box men. When I keep my eyes open to see if I can spot any, sure enough I see them roaming the streets, looking just the way the one did in the picture. But on the several occasions while I was observing them, I noticed that no one paid the slightest attention. It wasn't only my oversight. For example, suppose a box man goes up to a greengrocer's display. He stretches his arm out from a hole like this and begins pilfering stuff right and left in the area. Of course, only cheaper things without a price like tomatoes or milk or fermented soy beans. However, the clerk, dealing with a customer right beside the box man, far from scolding him, pretends not even to notice —pleasant, isn't it? You know what they say: 'Sweep the dust under the carpet.' Packing oneself up like baggage and walking about is an insult to the world and goes beyond just being strange behavior. Or was it so harmless an existence that one could overlook it by merely wishing to? You should be able to ignore me too if you want to."

The fake box man's words trailed off, and he stopped talking; I heaved a long sigh. As a condition perhaps it wasn't so bad. I more than anyone else knew full well that a box man lived a harmless existence. The location of the hospital was inconvenient, but since establishing himself the doctor had surely put aside a little nest egg; and then the very inconvenience of the location would serve to put a distance between us and the world. In the final analysis the question hung on her attitude alone. If she would only agree then perhaps the three of us could really make a go of it. No, no, not three, two and a little more. Treating him as a wastebasket would be stretching things, but if I considered him as a monkey I could keep him in a cage in my bedroom.

"Then it's all right with you?"

"With me?" She glanced quickly back at me and then just shifted her gaze toward the fake box man. As she did so, I felt a sharp jealousy at the smile that she let spread over her face. "It's beyond me. I'm not good at answering when I'm made to take responsibility. When I try thinking about it I'm always doing something strange like dropping a pair of scissors on my foot or sitting on a glass. I wonder what time it is now."

"Twenty-four minutes to ten," replied the fake box man, speaking rapidly, and I was made to feel guilty as if I were being blamed for my indecisiveness. She went right on, as if to press me.

"How old are you . . . really?"

"According to the official record twenty-nine, but actually thirty-two or -three, I guess."

Carried along, I answered in spite of myself, but apparently the question had not been what she really had intended to ask. Before I finished speaking, she had already turned her back to me and begun setting the instrument desk in order. Had she expressed without words that they had not yet decided on canceling examinations? Surely, arranging the instruments was a very normal thing to do. But she didn't seem all that serious about what she was doing. She simply appeared to be pushing the instruments and the glass containers here and there with her fingertips like model cars. Should I consider this a negative agreement? I wondered. If she did disagree, she would say so in so many words.

The fact that she had shown concern about the time could be an attempt to push me toward a decision. In short, I had the feeling that if I came to a definite resolution everything would be all right. If only I were to say the word and ask her to strip, at once the scene would change: two or three seconds of frantically unbuttoning the nacre buttons of her white tunic . . . and there she would be, naked before me. From where I was standing barely three yards away I could smell the very odor of her body, depending on the air currents in the room. But then would I be able to play, as they expected, the important role they had assigned me?

(An unpleasant recollection suddenly occurs to me. It concerns the student entertainment program in primary school. I was generally not popular and was thus assigned a trifling role, perhaps because no one else wanted it. It was the part of a horse by the name of Dunce, but for all of that I remember romping around in the greatest of high spirits. However, when it came time for me to go on stage, the short lines I was to deliver at only one point during the play would not come no matter how hard I tried to get them out. When I gave up and started to leave the stage, my classmate who played the role of the horse's owner, in an excess of anger, gave me a boot in the pants. That made me no less angry, and I kicked him back, whereupon he fell, struck his head on the floor, and lost consciousness. I have no recollection at all of how the play was subsequently discontinued. But it was soon after that that I became terribly nearsighted and squeezed some glasses out of my miserly parents. Myopia developed because I deliberately used to read books and magazines with fine print in dark places. I just wanted to run away from seeing and from being seen.)

I am quite aware of my own ugliness. I am not so shameless as to expose my nakedness nonchalantly before others. Of course, I'm not the only one who's unsightly: ninety-nine percent of mankind is deformed. It is my contention that man did not invent clothing after losing his hair, but that his hair atrophied because, aware of the unsightliness of his naked body, he tried to hide it with clothes. (I know very well that such an explanation goes against fact; yet I do believe it.) The reason men somehow go on living, enduring the gaze of others, is that they bargain on the hallucinations and the inexactitude of human eyes. By putting on clothes that as much as possible are identical and by having similar hairdos they manage to make it difficult to distinguish between one another. If I don't give a straight look, then the other person won't either; and one ends up leading a life of lowered glances. Thus long ago the punishment known as the pillory used to be used, but it was said to be too cruel and was discontinued in enlightened societies. That the act of spying on someone else is generally looked upon with scorn is because, I suppose, one does not want to be on the side of being seen. When one cannot avoid being seen it is common sense to demand compensation. As a matter of fact, in the theater or in the cinema usually those who look pay money and those who are looked at receive it. Anybody would rather look than be looked at. The fact that they keep on and on selling endless instruments for "looking"—radios and televisions—is excellent proof that ninety-nine percent of men are aware of their own unsightliness. I became nearsighted of my own accord, frequented strip houses, became an apprentice photographer . . . and from there it was but a step, and a most natural one, to being a box man.

> (Some marginal notes again in red ink. As for the existence of exhibitionism, I certainly have no bone

to pick with the claim of the author who considers visual rape to be a universal tendency in man. Time and again, exhibitionism tends to be confused with excessive sexual desire unsatisfied by the normal sexual act; but in fact there are many cases where it is overrepressed sexual expression. One patient, for example, made the following confession: His first condition for making the exhibitionistic act more effective is that the person he intends exhibiting himself to be unknown and of the other sex. Second, a fixed distance must be kept between him and the other person, and the relationship of seeing and of being seen must not be broken by approaching too close. Third, the two parties must not be able to distinguish each other's face. As a concrete case in which the preceding three conditions might be fulfilled, the patient suggested something like the inner courtyard of a girls' dormitory where there are numerous thickets. The tendency toward exhibitionism indicates that while the patient had a strong interest in the opposite sex generally, he had a morbid sense of shame concerning them individually, as they actually existed. According to the author's argument, this is the patient's realization of his ugliness. Further the patient said the following: In order to reach orgasm by the act of exhibitionism he would imagine receiving a sexual stimulus by the other party's seeing his sexual parts. If the other party clearly manifested her disgust that put a wet blanket on him, but to have her show curiosity was also irritating. To have the other party pretend that she didn't see him was by far the most stimulating. It was clearly a desire to have the other party participate in his exhibitionistic act as a visual rapist. Exhibitionism is merely the act of visual rape reflected in a mirror.)

"You're a vacillating fellow," said the fake box man, speaking rapidly in a tight, hard voice. "I would jump at the chance . . . something's wrong with you . . . such good conditions . . ."

"I hesitate because you get in my way."

"Ah . . . I see."

"Since I've had experience myself with being a box man, I think I know somewhat more about them than you. The reason the world ignores box men is because nobody understands who's inside the box. But your true colors are perfectly clear. I even know your way of looking at me. I don't like being stared at. I don't like it at all."

"But that's why I paid fifty thousand yen, isn't it?"

"I got used to looking, but I'm not yet accustomed to being looked at."

The fake box man swayed. After once bending diagonally forward, he arose with surprising agility. The back of the box rubbed against the wall and made a tawdry sound peculiar to dry cardboard. After all, something fake was something fake. It could not be compared with a genuine box long in use.

"Let's stop the idle talk now," cried the fake box man unsuitably cheerfully, stretching his legs. His bare limbs were sinewy and white and conspicuously hairy. I wondered if he were wearing no trousers. "I'm not exactly hungry, but *l'appetito viene mangiando*, you know." Then calling the girl's name, he ordered, "Come on, show him what you look like naked."

I was confused. Over and above the fact that she had suddenly been ordered to strip, I felt perplexed that she should be called by her own name. I hesitate even writing her name here and now. I am made to realize anew just how irreplaceable she is to me. Since she was the only person of the opposite sex that I had happened to meet, although that was pure chance, and since I had no one else to compare her with, one pronoun by which to distinguish the sexes would be plenty for me.

"Right now . . . right away?"

There was no particular hint of disapproval in her voice as she questioned him in return. She didn't even appear puzzled. Her answer gave one the feeling of caressing the curve of an egg with a palm smeared with facial cream. The way things were going now she would definitely be naked. I was nonplused, but I kept my mouth shut. My lips were paralyzed and I could not get a word out.

"It doesn't make any difference to you, does it?"

"No, but . . ."

A brief, businesslike exchange.

"It seems to me there were some matches over there, weren't there?"

Urged on by the fake box man, she slipped diagonally in front of me and crossed the room. Her gait was that of a small precision instrument that did not make one feel any wasted energy. She took a box of matches out of the pocket of her white tunic and flipped them with her finger-tips into the fake observation window. Suddenly I smelled her fragrance. It resembled the breezes flowing in from the fields of peanuts that one smelled on the seashore. The skin round my heart rippled. Was it jealousy directed against the fake box man? When she had turned adroitly aside and returned to her original position, she suddenly began un-buttoning the buttons on her white uniform. At the second button she casually looked at me. As the look was extremely light—it was as if it could float in space like a half day like that—far from averting my gaze, I managed to return her glance without blinking (this was important: if it was she looking, no matter how much she looked I had almost no feeling of being looked at). A light was lit in the lamp of her expression. The line of her eyebrows softened faintly, and her teeth were visible between moist lips. It was an open expression. Were the doors open for me? She went on . . . the third button. Then the fourth. If she really tries to understand me completely, if she intends to catch me with the posture she showed to the fake box man last night, then surely I need nothing like a box. Others' unsightliness should be invisible to those who have no unsightliness of their own to hide. If a box man is a specialized voyeur, then she is a born victim of that voyeur (the only worrisome thing is why the doctor, faced with this aspect of her, was made to feel he should live in a box). Then the last button. . . .

Fortunately she was not at once naked under her white uniform, and I finally regained my composure. A blouse of orange silk fitted close to her skin. There was a line of tiny buttons of the same color, like grass seeds. A short yellow-ocher skirt held at the side by three black buttons about three-fourths of an inch in diameter. I heard the sound of a match being struck in the box. I had assumed that the color of her skin was on the light side, but in contrast with the shade of her skirt it was rather swarthy. Yet her fingers, poised on the buttons of the skirt, were definitely light. As I looked I could no longer tell, actually, which was true. Her fingers once poised on the skirt, hesitated, changed their mind, and shifted to the grass seeds on her blouse. Ah ha, of course she should start from there. As for me, I wanted more time. I began to smell a cigarette. For example, she whom I had happened to meet the week before—she who unsuspecting as a child had wiped away all my debts like some high-powered, all-purpose cleaning device —if it were she alone it was possible that I might happen on her again somewhere. In any case I would apparently have the opportunity of meeting the one whom I had spied on last night, she who was so tolerant of others' unsightliness, who was like a device for freeing me of desire that made me forget my sense of inferiority like a drug or alcohol. Although it was a fact, it was difficult to believe at a moment's notice that the two had come together in a single personality. Of course, as far as she was concerned, I did not yet know her well enough to be able to express any opinion that smacked of criticism. What use was it, I wondered, for the right eye to know about the left? The essential thing is trust where very naturally one shares concern with another, where one can observe things without any particular consciousness. She undid the third grass-seed button. Under her blouse she was apparently naked. Although I could smell a cigarette I could not see any smoke. It was wrong to smoke like that. In the meantime smoke suddenly began to waft out from the cracks in the box and from the observation window, filling the inside so that anyone in there would not be able to keep his eyes open.

"Are you about ready?" said the fake box man triumphantly. "Look, she doesn't pay any attention to me at all."

The girl smiled slightly as she undid the fifth button. It was a faltering smile. There were still seven grass seeds left to go.

"It's all right if you want to take pictures."

I was taken by surprise. To be sure she had promised to model for me. Even though she had stripped, there was no reason for me to do the same. I had nothing against taking my clothes off, but there was no need to do so on the spot. I seemed arbitrarily to be worrying unnecessarily. In an effort to ease the awkwardness of the situation I reached into my tote bag (it was in the basket I put my clothes in when I took them off), which contained my camera, but in the end gave that idea up. If I set my camera up here and now, I would be tacitly recognizing a life in common with the box man. That might be better than stripping my clothes off, but after all it was like handing over a passkey to my private room.

"This background is impossible."

As she undid the seventh button, she twisted the upper part of her body and looked at the wall behind her. The neck of her collar opened and I could see her brassière. It was a dark gray with exposed seams like those on a rugby ball. Indeed, perhaps the setting was tasteless. There were a glass case and lines of sterile instruments. A very narrow examination couch. An enamel washbasin supported by slender, curved, metal legs. And then a weird mechanical seat that resembled a dentist's chair, but that somehow had a different feeling. That was what made it interesting. There was an eroticism in this assortment as in pictures of hell. I supposed then that if I had plenty of film and when the sun moved a little over to the south, I should ultimately not be able to resist the seduction of taking some pictures.

"If you wish we can shift places. I'll go over there," said the fake box man obligingly.

"No, no, that won't do at all. I'll be against the light."

Quiet! Quiet! If I talk here I'll end up by confessing. Her fingers went to the ninth button; if she undoes the remaining three buttons the blouse will slip off.

"From what I have observed about you, you would prefer more direct action than just taking pictures," he said with false vivacity. The fake box man began to putty over the space left open by my silence with random chatter. "If I had the choice I would prefer direct action too. Let's stop saying she doesn't excite us. You can take pictures any time; it's like being told to hold off at the crucial point. You don't have to pay any attention to me. I long ago waived my rights to her. It must already be about a year now. . . . Our affair began with her coming to have an abortion. After the operation was over, as she had no money, she asked me unexpectedly to let her pay me back by working. With that innocent face . . . I was surprised . . . but anyway at such times one comes to a decision amazingly fast . . . surprisingly so. Properly, I did not inquire into the name of the man or about her relatives. I tried to hold her by ignoring her past."

"If you had asked me, I would have told you."

"I don't particularly mean I intentionally didn't ask."

"Anyway I was glad you didn't."

"The nurse who had been here up until then didn't put a very good face on it. She called you a saucy minx."

"How did *you* think of me?"

"At first I thought you were terribly suspicious of people. Then I thought you were perhaps overly trusting. You do everything so impulsively. Furthermore when you're scolded you at once admit your mistake with equal simplicity. You seem to believe that just by recognizing your errors any misdeed is erased."

"Was I all that bother?" Her fingers were poised on the last button.

"No. Everything's erased. When I think back on it now my intuition not to try to question you about your past was pretty good. And knowing you, you could have taken to your heels without leaving a trace . . . even if you had walked on freshly fallen snow."

She laughed briefly with the tips of her tightly pursed lips, and when she pulled the tails of the blouse, which she had finished unbuttoning, from her skirt, she let it slip to her fingertips and flung it with two fingers onto one end of the examination couch. A number of narrow pleats gathered at the stricture of her waist as she twisted. Although she did not appear to be especially thin, the layer of subcutaneous fat seemed scanty. That set up some association of ideas, but what was it now? Oh, yes, the feel of the soft chamois skin that I wiped my lenses with.

"But we were able to get along rather well, weren't we?"

"We did too well!" said the fake box man in a nasal voice, scornful of himself. "But I'm an easily satisfied rascal. I arbitrarily assumed that I had the power to keep her. I'm the weird one. I would shave twice a day, morning and night. I acted like a seducer. Further, since our relationship was one of doctor and a patient who had come for a D and C, we could talk about her uterus and her clitoris as if we were discussing the ripeness of figs in the garden. Our relationship after that went like Newton's apple . . . and the law of gravity. The nurse I had had up until then promptly upped and left."

(There is a marginal entry in red ink and an arrow marks the insertion between these lines.

"I didn't know the nurse who left was your wife, for heaven's sake."

"It wouldn't have made any difference if you had. She was thoroughly fed up with her part.")

"I don't like to see anyone hurt."

"Hm. I wonder . . . When was it that I asked you . . . ? If it were established that the world were going to end, I wanted to know if you would spend the last moment together with me. You answered that if you could you would like to spend it alone looking at the sea."

"Liar! I must have said I'd like to be with as many people as I possibly could . . . someplace like a station, a department store . . . a bustling place."

"It comes to about the same thing."

"I can't believe that the world will come to an end so simply."

"Anyway I've got you to pay what you owe me. You don't owe another yen."

The yellow skirt became a tube and slipped to the floor at her feet. Standing over it on her left leg, she hooked it with the tip of her right foot and propelled it lightly into the air. The skirt described an unexpectedly heavy movement and fell to the floor on the near side of the examination couch. The buttons clicked against each other, making a sound as if someone were treading on little mussels. Incredibly tiny sheer blue panties cut into the flesh of her hips. She bent her legs slightly and put the flat of her hands on the outer sides of her thighs. It resembled the posture of one about to dive into water, but there was a more comical feeling to it. One by one her movements made creases in space, brought about a chiaroscuro, created currents, and carved out a whole new world. I was stricken by a wretchedness as if suddenly catching a cold. It was a kind of feeling of jealousy at seeing all these things for the first time.

"Just a minute," interrupted the fake box man just as she put her fingers on the band of her panties. She stopped moving, looking somewhere into the distance beyond my head.

"Say, you're almost not looking at her at all. After all you're the one she took her clothes off for. Use those eyes of yours, man, and feel her up. Do you know those figurines made of white rice-flour paste? That's the feeling I get from the stretch from her neck to her arms . . . it's a flowing sensation as in the elongated paste just before it gets hard. But what I like best is the curve that runs from her waist to the swelling of her buttocks. Somewhere a little something still remains of a girl's body before she blossoms into womanhood."

"Well, as far as I'm concerned, I like her legs best." As I said this, my jaw suddenly stiffened and my teeth ground together. My eyeballs were heavy, and I was unable to raise my eyes to her face. What, I wondered, would her expression be now? Nevertheless, I was suspicious about the fact that there was no sign of cigarette smoke rising from the box, nor did the fake box man even begin to cough. "But I don't understand . . . well-shaped legs, poorly shaped legs . . . it's like being forced to read a foreign language I am unacquainted with. Why do I cling so to legs? I myself find it strange."

"It's because they're closest to the sexual parts."

"I don't agree. If that were true then any leg would do the trick. I wonder if it doesn't have something to do with flight, running away. I am tempted to chase after legs that look fast for running away."

"Pretty far-fetched, don't you think? She's not running away, she's waiting. Shall I tell you what's wrong? You're too far away. Since you won't try taking a half pace forward, you can't even lift your face. And I'm going to tell you just why you can't take that half step forward." The fake box man cleared his voice and left the corner where he had been standing; he shifted his position to the tip of the isosceles triangle whose base formed the line connecting her with me. "Fish, birds, animals—all engage in strange courtship ceremonies before mating. According to specialists, it's apparently a modified form of attack and threat. All living things have their individual area of influence, and they demonstrate an instinctive reaction in attacking any encroaching invader. But mating would never come about if you based yourself on the single principle of attack no matter what. Since coupling is the contact of epiderms, it will never take place unless somewhere the boundary lines are broken or some door is opened. Therefore, in mating, by a modified movement or gesture that at first glance resembles attack but that somehow is different, a technique is born

When I look at small things, I think I shall go on
living: drops of rain . . . leather gloves shrunk
by being wet . . . When I look at something
too big, I want to die: the Diet Building . . .
or a map of the world . . . or . . .

by which the protective instinct of the other party is scrambled or made to relax. It's the same for humans. We talk about romance, but this is after all merely aggressive instinct camouflaged with makeup and feathers. Whichever it is, it doesn't change the fact that the ultimate purpose lies in breaking down and disregarding the lines of demarcation of a given area. From my own experience the line in the case of humans seems to be located at a radius of about two and a half yards. Courting is good, making the other party hesitate with sparkling beads and all that is good; anyway when you get through that line of demarcation you have already taken possession. At this very close proximity it is difficult rather than easy, as one would expect, to distinguish the true character of the enemy. Only touch and smell are of any use."

"When all's said and done, what do you mean?"

"If you take a half pace forward, you'll be right on that line."

"So what?"

"You're a vacillating fellow, aren't you. You've gone to the trouble of getting the girl to make you out a *laissez-passer* over the demarcation line, haven't you? If you go another half pace forward, like it or not, you will be asked to present that *laissez-passer*. It's a free pass, of course. Naturally when you use it, you at once waive any pretext, any right to go back to the box. You're frightened of recognizing that. You're marking time because you're afraid. You've got her tied hand and foot, there, see? You've sealed off time."

When I considered what he had said, I could see that it was quite true. She had made almost no movement from the tentative position in which she had poised her fingers on the elastic of her panties. Her eyes, vaguely fixed in space as if seeking something beyond my head, remained wide open like artificial ones.

"What's wrong?"

"Ah . . . 'There's no villain among those who hate news'? I wonder," snorted the fake box man, slurring the ends of his words. "Aren't you, who don't believe in change, being inconsistent? You're afraid of getting what you yourself asked for, and so you're stopping time."

"Such a feat is impossible, I should say."

"I read the story of the fellow who stuffed his mistress and lived with her that way. He says that a stuffed mistress is a lot more faithful than a real live one and a lot more sexy."

"Unfortunately I don't have those tastes."

"That's perfectly all right. That's the conclusion we have come to, isn't it? Anyway the only thing that's clear is that you don't want to get out of the box."

"I've told you, I disposed of the box before I came here."

"Well, then, let me just ask, at this very moment what are you doing and where are you doing it?"

"As you yourself can see. I'm chatting with you . . . here."

"I see. If that is true, who is writing these notes and where are they writing them? Then it wasn't someone writing in a box by the light of a naked bulb in a dressing room by the sea?"

"Oh, that's something better left unsaid. If you talk about it you yourself will admit that you two are merely figments of my imagination."

"Hm . . . I wonder."

"It's indisputable."

"Of course, only one of the three of us really exists. The one who is in fact continuing to write these notes. Everything that has happened is merely the monologue of that someone. Even you must recognize that. At the rate things are going, this someone intends to go on writing forever and ever in order to cling desperately to the box."

"You're too suspicious. I'm just waiting for my underclothes to dry. As soon as they are, I intend to leave at once. I scrubbed myself so hard that when the wind blows on my skin it tingles. I've just stayed in the box to get out of the wind for a while. There's no particular reason for me to have any lingering affection for notes like these. I'll stop at once. I'll make this the last line I write."

"When your underclothes are dry do you really intend to come to see us?"

"I say I made preparations to visit you, but from the first I arranged for very little baggage. Strictly speaking, I need just one thing in order to get out of the box. But it's indispensable. I can't leave the box if I don't have it—do you understand? A pair of trousers. If I were just in trousers, somehow I could go out into the world. It would make no difference whether I was naked from the waist up and my feet bare just as long as I had trousers on. Otherwise if you go walking around the streets without trousers, no matter how new your shoes and how elegant your coat, it's enough to raise a big hue and cry. Enlightened society is a kind of trouser society. Fortunately I have made provision for what is to come and have prepared for future use a new pair of trousers only. When I came for treatment last week I was wearing them for the first time. If you use them as padding at the ceiling of the box, they don't get in the way. And then a professional camera . . . and other things not especially important. If they're troublesome I have no regrets about tossing them out. No, I don't have to throw them away, I can turn them over to you. Toiletries, safety-razor blades, matches, paper cup, earplugs, thermos bottle, a rear-view mirror for a car, waterproof rubber tape . . . paregoric, eyewash, Mercurochrome, and so forth, but these may be omitted since you're a doctor and already have them . . . six photos cut out of Volume Two of *A Collection of Modern Nude Photographic Masterpieces* and a tube for looking at them . . . as far as instructions for use are concerned, you'll understand as soon as you try using it . . . and then, besides a pocket flashlight, a ballpoint pen and other sundries like a plastic board or a ring of wire and items of daily use it is difficult to describe. They seem to be trifling things, but they form a necessary and efficient living set endorsed by the experience of box living. I do not mean to put you in my debt, but I think this set a suitable parting gift for a new box man. And then it would be well perhaps to have a miniature radio for a while at first. Aside from being afflicted with total news addiction as I was, one is periodically overwhelmed, until one gets used to it, by an unspeakable sense of loneliness."

"Really, when do you expect your washing will be dry?"

"It's just stopped raining and the air's pretty moist. They're half dry, and when its gets light and the direction of the wind changes it won't take long."

"Then you mean that it's still dark where you are?"

"See there, there's something flashing around the horizon line and the sea. The squid boats are heaving to, I expect. It's just about time for them. It'll be light soon."

"I don't care if your clothes aren't completely dry. Put them on anyway, don't be persnickety. Even the urine-stained shorts will dry by themselves while you've got them on. If you don't hurry up, we'll get tired of waiting."

"I feel as if I've caught a cold. Perhaps it's because I haven't had enough sleep, but my feet feel hot and I'm having chills. It feels good when I bury my legs in the sand, but it's cold. Maybe I took too long in the shower. When I went to your hospital last week, my wound was hurting me terribly and I couldn't wash thoroughly, but I intended

here and now to get completely rid of the three years' ac-
cumulation of dirt. I used up a whole new bar of soap. I just
wanted to show it to you, it was special soap. I had plenty
of time, or rather I suppose the work at hand tended to
absorb me, because during this week I had many things to
think about. I tried sculpting her torso. Just a woman's torso,
because it was quite beyond my capabilities to make it look
like hers. I put some nostril hairs at her crotch, and though
I tried to sculpt her absolutely realistically, frankly it resembled a frog more than a woman. Well, aside from the
shape it was now in, the soap was a good brand and of the
best quality. First I wet myself completely in the shower,
then soaped myself all over, and scrubbed myself hard with
my underwear in place of a washcloth. Then after I had
scraped away with my nails until I hurt, I showered off.
When I had repeated this four times, the darkish rinse water
turned clear. The fourth time I washed my hair, a lot of
what seemed to be bubbles began to rise. But after that
everything went wrong. What I was looking forward to was
the sensation of passing my fingers over a polished glass
after having taken a long bath and got rid of the grease. It
wouldn't work. In the meantime the soap had wasted away
and could no longer be used, my arms were heavy and would
not rise, and my whole body smarted as if a thin layer of
skin had been stripped off. I felt like retching. Anyway perhaps it was an error to try to get rid of three years' worth of
dirt with just one cake of soap. Perhaps I had become a pile
of dirt, except for my bones. As soon as I flopped down
exhausted on the sand, I heard from above me what sounded
like a gravel truck falling down. It was nothing. Only the
motor to the pump. I was defeated. If I took another three
years, with the brinish water from the well dug directly on the
seashore, I would never get the soap off."

"Which one of us will give up first? The one who

wears out talking or the one who wears out listening?"

"Ah! I've finally come to realize who you really are. I thought that the way you expressed yourself was simply too clever . . . a simple product of imagination. Saying you were not a product of my imagination would not particularly raise you in standing. This examination room itself, including yourselves, is the scribbling on the walls of my box. Simply scribblings. Judging from your box, you can't imagine it, I suppose, but there's a difference between a genuine and a fake box. I am now actually looking at that closed-off room big enough for just one person. The inside of a face that no one can imitate since no one can see it, a collection of graffiti written compactly all over the inner cardboard walls tanned by three years of sweat and sighs . . . this is the story of my life . . . there is a sketch map of the town for the purpose of collecting foodstuffs as well as memoranda for the purpose of these notes. Besides all this, ciphers and diagrams the sense of which I myself do not clearly apprehend. Everything I need is here."

"What time is it now by your watch?"

"Ah . . . eight minutes . . . of five."

"You started writing on the beach at exactly three eighteen, didn't you? It's a weird watch. I figure that since you began, only an hour and thirty-four minutes have gone by."

"It would be better for you not to forget that you are merely my scribblings. You say that I tend to cling too much to the box? As soon as I dispose of it as you advise, you too will completely disappear with the scribblings."

"You're rather an optimist."

"And thanks to you I rather dislike myself."

"See . . . the pages of your notes come to fifty-nine. Fifty-nine pages in an hour and thirty-four minutes. No matter how you look at it, that's impossible, I should say.

How many times did I warn you? You're too long-winded. I'd like you to remember what you've done up until now. How many pages could you average an hour? Normally not even a page. When you were writing at your fastest the best you ever covered was four pages. And they were written in a horrible scribble."

"There have been times when I could write more."

"Well, then, shall we compromise and say that you can write five pages an hour? Fifty-nine pages divided by five makes eleven, leaving four. Eleven hours and fifty minutes, shall we say? Since these are your last pages, it comes roughly to twelve hours, wouldn't you agree? A total of twelve hours of constant writing without food or drink. If you began at three in the morning, it would be absolutely impossible for it to be now something before three in the afternoon."

"May I remind you that these are my notes. Whatever way I write them it is purely up to me."

"Perhaps it is, in certain circumstances. Maybe, for example, you wrote all this nonsense for some reason I don't know. Or maybe over twenty-four hours went by while you were unconscious. Or maybe the rotation of the earth was put out of kilter by some natural calamity. But if you go so far as to claim that, then I can set forth a completely different hypothesis. Yes, quite different. There's no need to claim that you are the author of these notes. Because there's absolutely no problem even if the author is someone other than yourself."

"Stop these false charges. I am actually writing. The seashore's dark and enveloped in the smell of the sea. Right overhead tiny insects swarm like smoke around the naked, filthy light bulb in the bathhouse. For some reason when they fall on my box they make a sound that resembles raindrops, so I realize they're larger than I thought. Now I put a cigarette to my lips, strike a match, the flame lights my naked knees, I approach the burning tip of the cigarette to my knees and look—I clearly feel the heat. These are realities that no one can doubt. If I were to stop writing here and now, no other character, not another line would appear."

"Hm . . . Then perhaps someone different is writing in some other place."

"Who?"

"Me, for example. . . ."

"You . . . ?"

"Yes, perhaps I'm the one writing. Perhaps it is I who am going on writing as I imagine you who are writing as you imagine me."

"What for?"

"For indicting the box man. Maybe I'm trying to impress on people that he really exists."

"That's an unexpected turnabout. If we suppose that you are the author, then the box man becomes simply a figment of the imagination."

"Well, then, suppose I am trying to impress on you the fact that he doesn't actually exist in order to prove his irreality."

"Ah, indeed. I wondered if that weren't it. I had a premonition. But no matter how many tricks you try, they are destined to be futile. Because I have material proof. Yes, perhaps I should have warned you ahead of time before entering into negotiations. If you know that I am not unarmed, even you won't act rashly. No, I have no intention of putting that proof to bad use; if I had I would have done so long ago. If only you would show your sincerity. I'll give you all the material evidence later."

"I'm sorry, but I've no idea what you're trying to suggest."

"Please. I feel quite dizzy from lack of sleep just doing

nothing. Well, then, let me tell you. Who was it, I wonder, who shot me with an air rifle? I've got my eye on someone."

"A lot of people have air rifles in this neighborhood. The weasels apparently wreak havoc in the chicken houses," she suddenly said again, repeating the same excuse. Creakingly, somehow time began to move. I did not wish to hurt the girl, but I found it unpardonable that she should side with the fake box man.

"Unfortunately there's unshakable proof, you know. The instant I was hit, I at once snapped the shutter—a professional reflex. I saw the developed picture that very day. I had made a good shot. It was a back picture of someone busily going up the sloping road, concealing a rifle by trying to fit it to the length of his body under his arm. The way he cut his hair, the new made-to-order suit fitted to his round shoulders, the conspicuous wrinkles in his trousers, nonetheless of the best material, and the distinctive low shoes like slippers." Then my tone changed to a plain and simple one, and I addressed myself exclusively to her: "Shall we play a little guessing game? Some profession where one is constantly taking off and putting on shoes, one where there is often the opportunity of sitting in Japanese fashion, one belonging to the financially upper classes, one where one can wear one's hair without worrying what others think. What would you guess? I don't think it's all that hard. Anybody would immediately think of a doctor on house calls, wouldn't he? Furthermore, it happens that the mounting road I photographed was right next to the soy factory at the foot . . ."

At this point events suddenly took an abrupt turn. The fake box man—the fake box man who until then had stood straight upright merely expressionless, harmless, like a trash can that had sprouted legs—began to shake his box awkwardly, making an annoying sound. The vinyl curtain over the observation window separated, and from within a long stick was thrust out. It was an air rifle. Aimed straight at my left eye.

"Stop it!" I parried in a casual tone, half jokingly. "I seem to have a touch of phobia for extremities, a weakness in me. So pointing at me like that . . ."

"Won't you show me the film?"

"I didn't bring it along. It's my only trump that will guarantee me an equal right to speak."

"Search him!" the fake box man urged her in a shrill voice.

She hesitated. Entreatingly she looked up at me. With her hands clasped at her breast and seeming to push up the collar of her dress, she began to shift her balance forward. Whereupon the front of her white ironed tunic (had she put it on sometime without my realizing it?) gaped wide open. Only the topmost button was fastened. Under the white dress she was naked. I had half expected that, but I was taken by surprise. The nakedness under the white garment gave the feeling of a nakedness stripped more naked than ordinary. The white dress was not a white dress, but had turned into the ceremonial garment of a sacrificial victim. The strong curved skin surfaces, uniformly taut, were suggestive of some strange machine I did not understand. The narrow jaw and the roundness of her belly alone did not suit her and were childlike. I wracked my brain. As in someone else's briefcase, the disorder in my head was extreme. Her left leg moved forward, trying to support the leaning weight. At once my field of vision contracted, and I felt aggressive. I myself did not understand why.

"All right, I'll do it myself. It's not worth bothering yourself with." I went to the box in the corner by the door in which I had put my clothes when they were removed, opened the neck of a mountain-climbing bag (probably an American Army surplus item), and fished out a stuffed toy crocodile. "As far as I'm concerned I'm lucky just to find that you feel guilty. I had the feeling your conditions were simply too good to be true."

The crocodile that I took out was a little less than eighteen inches in length, the circumference of the torso sixteen and a half; it was a toy crocodile painted green with inset plastic eyeballs and fangs, a warty back, claws of light brown, and a red, snapping mouth. Anyone looking at this merry, overly innocent doll would surely have his fighting ardor dampened. A child's toy usually makes the average adult lose his hostility unless he has a morbid dislike of children. In view of my psychological tendencies, this was not an ordinary doll. The crocodile was a blackjack that I had invented. I do not refer to cards, but to the blackjack, the deadly weapon that has gained notoriety by being favored principally by the Mafia and the secret police. I take the shavings and spongy filling out and usually carry around just the outside bag, but this morning I had a premonition and in advance stuffed it with sand from the beach. If you take hold of the tail end and just give it a shake, you feel how really dangerous it can be. If you strike with all your force you crush the skull. Of course, there's no need to go about things so enthusiastically. You can attack someone fatally and yet leave no outer wound; that's the good feature of the blackjack. When you've finished using it, you unfasten the end and scatter the sand that comes out around the garden. If there's any trouble it would never occur to anyone that a crocodile skin could be used as a dangerous weapon.

Pretending to give the crocodile to the fake box man with some reluctance, I struck from below at the end of the gun barrel. The destructive power was unimaginable from the speed. The rifle barrel bit into the upper frame of the window, and the box jumped. An angry groan came from the doctor, who had been taken by surprise. At the same time I heard the sound of air escaping, as if someone had driven a nail into a bicycle tire. The bullet had gone up toward the ceiling, but the sound of it hitting could not be heard. I wrested the gun from his grasp. The doctor, not to be out-done, thrust his arm out the observation window. He clutched my right cheek like a rice cake, and with unexpected power I brought the sandbag crocodile down on my oppo-nent's farther shin. There was a damp and heavy sound as of a hatchet biting into unseasoned wood. Uttering a shriek, the doctor drew his arm back into the box. I broke out in sweat at the vociferations that ran the gamut of the vowels. I began striking at the head at the top of the box to try to make him stop and then paused. I did not want to hurt the box. I con-tinued to beat at his farther shin, this time taking more care (I would be in something of a fix if he were able to remain in the hospital under the pretext of broken bones). The doctor squeezed himself up into a small ball and became perfectly passive like the wastebasket he had said he was. If he had not groaned like an empty pipe, I should never have thought a man was hiding inside the box. At first I looked at the box expressionlessly. The wan ten-o'clock sun flowing in from the window melted into the white of the mortar wall, filling the room, and in it the box seemed like a scooped-out hole.

Supposing that it is not I who am pushing on with these notes now (I too cannot help but recognize the contradiction in time that has been pointed out by the fake box man), and whoever it may be, I think he has an extremely stupid way of advancing the story line. If he has come this far the next scene can only be one thing in any case. I turn and look at the girl. What attitude does the author intend to have her take now? Depending on how she reacts to me, the outcome, how-ever pleasant or unpleasant it may be, will make clear what I have gained and what I have lost by giving up the box. For example, is she going to accept me like that with the buttons of her white dress unbuttoned, or with them buttoned up? No, it is hardly suitable to make the buttons the measurement of her attitude. But out of amazement she may forget to button them up, and on the other hand she may well button them up once to accept me formally and not abridge the ceremony of unbuttoning them. Thus as long as I stay beyond the two-and-a-half-yard line as I am, it will surely be easy to read her expression. If an unconcealable look of relief shows through her tense expression, that will mean that her relationship has, from the first, been one of estrangement with the doctor and that I will rescue her from his high-handedness and restraint; but if, on the contrary, she is afraid of accepting me, that will show that the two have been accomplices from the beginning and that I shall have to escape from this tiger's den.

Enough. Whichever it was it was indescribable ridiculousness. The objectionable thing was not so much the lack of logic but rather the fact that in all these happenings everything was so smooth. The truth was more fragmented, like a picture puzzle with many pieces missing and filled with flights of imagination. Although I am perhaps not I, was it necessary for me to go on living and going to the trouble of writing these notes? I may seem to be repeating, but a box man is an ideal victim. If I had been the doctor I should have at once offered a cup of tea. Being a doctor, it would be easy for him to slip in a drop of poison. Or . . . perhaps . . . had I already been made to drink the cup of tea? I wondered. Perhaps I had. It was possible. Certainly there was absolutely no proof that I was still alive.

AFFIDAVIT

All statements made are truthful. Since you ask about the corpse washed up at T Seaside Park, I make herewith a detailed deposition of my own volition, concealing nothing.

Name: C.
Permanent address: Omitted.
Profession: Doctor's assistant (orderly).
Date of Birth (day, month, year): 7 March 1927.

My real name is C, but the full one I use when I practice medicine and the one registered at the Bureau of Public Health is the name of the army surgeon who was my superior officer when I joined the colors as a medical corpsman during the war. I used it with the permission of the officer in question.

I have never yet been condemned for crime to penal servitude nor have I even been questioned as a suspect by the police or the public prosecutor.

I have never been a public servant nor have I ever received any decoration, relief funds, or pension.

I am still unmarried, but in point of fact, concerning my family, until last year I have been living with my common-law wife, Nana, who helped me as a nurse in my work and was in charge of all accounts. Originally Nana was the legal wife of the army doctor whose name and identity I borrowed while I was practicing, but since I was cohabiting with her with the doctor's understanding and approbation there was never any trouble. Until last year there was no conspicuous disharmony between Nana and me, but when I hired Toyama Yoko as a new apprentice nurse, Nana was not happy and suggested we live apart. I agreed, and until now that is what we have been doing.

During the war I discharged my military duties as a medical corpsman, and, putting that experience to good use, I engaged in practice on my own. I enjoyed a good reputation among the patients, and I have never requested instructions or help from a regularly licensed doctor. My special proficiency lies mainly in the area of surgery such as appendectomies. If I am blamed for illegal practice I shall reconsider using another's name; I shall make amends to the world and promise never to engage in medical work again.

Now I shall discuss the corpse, the cause of whose death is unknown, that you ask about. . . .

The Case of C

Now you are writing.

A dark room where the lights have been turned off with the exception perhaps of the lamp on the worktable. At just this instant you raise your head from the affidavit you are in the act of writing and have just drawn a deep breath. When, in the same position, you turn your neck diagonally to the right, a thin line of light runs over the right edge of the desk. It is a beam seeping in under the door from the corridor. If someone were to pass by, like it or not, his shadow could not help but be inscribed on that line. You wait. Seven seconds, eight . . . there is no sign of anyone.

On the old white door the layers of paint cannot conceal the surface scratches. Staring at the door, you think of many things. What is that sound that catches your attention now? Is it only your fancy? Yes, you hear it . . . there . . . that's it . . . from a different direction. You look around at the window. A movable house of cardboard precisely modeled on the one worn by the box man on the bed next to the wall. Has the real box man at last taken it into his head to come? No, the interval between footfalls is too short. It is not a dog either. Perhaps it is that chicken. It is that weird hen that sometime learned to walk about at night. Every night she wanders around here, searching for food. Is a night-prowling chicken an extremely strange phenomenon or not? Since it can monopolize all the night insects that crawl out unafraid, there is plenty of food and it should be well fed, but it is thin and sickly. If one finds oneself with exceptional talents one has to pay unexpected compensation (you seem to be taking a lesson from the chicken now).

You try lifting to your lips the half-drunk glass of beer. You decide to stop with just wetting the tip of your tongue a little. The beer is completely flat and undrinkable. More than four hours have already passed since you sat down here. Although it will soon be the end of September, the weather is depressing. You stop the sweat that flows from the hairline at your forehead with some cotton soaked in alcohol and moisten your sticky lips with saliva, but you cannot very well turn on the fan or the air conditioner. You must not miss hearing whatever footfalls there may be. You have become terribly suspicious.

A thick slab of glass lies on the desk. On it the half-written affidavit. The affidavit concerning the incident that has not yet taken place and that we are sure will. Pushing it

The white tiles are bespeckled with spots the color of dried leaves, and notched in them are grooves to prevent slipping. A thin line of water undulates gently along the grooves. For a moment it forms a little puddle, then begins to flow again, and disappears under the door.

aside, you open a notebook. Quarto size, lined with orange-colored horizontal lines . . . This is surprising; I did not know that you had even prepared notes exactly like mine. You absently turn the cover. The first page begins with the following sentence:

> *"This is the record of a box man. I am at this time beginning to write this record in my box. I am in a cardboard box that fits over my head and covers me completely to the hips.*
>
> *"That is, at this point, the box man is my very self."*

You flip over more than ten pages and open to a clean one. Grasping your ballpoint pen, you assume a posture for writing, but changing your mind, you look at your watch. Still nine minutes until midnight. The last Saturday in September is just coming to a close. You rise from your seat, pen and notebook in hand. You walk to the bed. You tilt the box over diagonally and crawl in, bringing it down over your head from the back. You present a figure seated on the edge of the bed with the box over your head. Apparently you have become rather used to getting in and out of the box. You adjust it so that the observation window is directed at the lamp on the desk. But there is not enough light to take notes. You switch on the flashlight suspended over the observation window. Making the plastic board you have provided into a table, you begin taking your notes on that.

> *"The following is a summary of the incident: The place is the city of T, the last Monday in September . . ."*

You evidently fancy to begin recording the past events of the day after tomorrow when nothing has yet occurred. What is the hurry? Or is it that you are backed up by your considerable self-confidence? Since you are trying to establish a chronology of actions that you describe in the past tense, evidently those actions had already been going on when I began reading these notes. You already were aware of the results of those actions, though I was not, for you could make an educated guess. But I should like to read right on in your notes. I cannot believe that there was any other clear purpose for the action than to bring death.

You begin to write.

> *"On the outskirts of a little frequented seaside park, an unidentified body was washed up. The body was wearing over its head a box made of packing cardboard, secured by a cord tied around its waist. Undoubtedly it was a box man who had been wandering about the city lately and who, by mistake, had fallen into a canal; the body was swept by the tides onto the beach. Other than the box, he had no possessions. The result of the autopsy made it possible to set the supposed time of death about thirty hours previously."*

Thirty hours previously . . . you were very decisive about that. Let us suppose for the moment that the time of the autopsy was early in the morning of Monday. Going back thirty hours from then puts us at precisely the present moment. At the latest it will be within several hours from now. You too have evidently made up your mind to face death. When you hastily close your notes, you slip off the bed and kneel on the floor. You shove the box, which has dipped forward, off toward the back. The things inside the box knock against each other and set up a din. Confused, you hug the box to you, looking over your shoulder. You look up, straining your ears to catch any noise beyond the walls, beyond the ceiling. Fear paints a streak of varnish down your face. The varnish is evidently quick-drying, and the surface of your face is covered with crepelike wrinkles. You are much too nervous.

Why can't you be more practical? You can only do what you can no matter how you try.

You straighten up and face the door. You begin to walk. You hold your elbows close to your sides; and your fingers, all together, slightly bend inward. You take three steps and your strength leaves you. You change directions and go in front of the desk. Seating yourself, you hold your head in your arms. The notes that you have placed between your elbow and your side slip noiselessly onto the desk. And then time indolently goes by as you think.

You are now staring at the edge of the thick glass plate on top of the desk. A pure blue that doesn't belong anywhere, that has no feeling of distance between its two surfaces. An infinite greenish blue. A dangerous color, filled with the blue temptations of flight. You drown in the blue. When your body sinks out of sight in it, you look as if you will go on swimming forever. You recall the many times you have had this temptation. The blue of the wake welling up from a steamship propeller . . . the stagnant water of an abandoned sulphur mine . . . blue pellets of rat poison that resemble jelly candy . . . the violet dawn that one sees, waiting for the first train with no place to go . . . it is the colored glass of the spectacles of love distributed by the Suicide Aid Society, or if you wish, the Spiritual Euthanasia Club. The glass is tinted with the thin membrane of a wan winter sun that a skilled technician strips away with great care. Only those who wear these glasses can see the terminus from which the one-way train sets out.

I wonder if perhaps you are not too engrossed with the box. Perhaps you are poisoned by the box, which is merely a means. I hear that the box is indeed a dangerous source of blue.

> *The color of rain that gives beggars colds . . . The*
> *color of the hour when the store shutters of the*

*underground passages are drawn . . . the color of
the graduation watch forfeited to the pawnbroker
. . . the color of jealousy broken on the stainless
steel sink of the kitchen . . . the color of the first
morning of unemployment . . . the color of the
ink of a useless I.D. card . . . the color of the last
movie ticket the candidate for suicide purchases
. . . the color of the hole that has been eaten away
by hours of such strong alkalinity as anonymity,
hibernation, euthanasia.*

But by shifting my gaze only a few inches, you are already outside the hole. No matter how serious you pretend to be you are after all a fake box man. You can't stop yourself from being what you are. You are now looking at a calendar from a pharmaceutical company, that you have laid under the plate glass on the desk. Monthly slogans are printed on it: to the left, "The Season for Vitamins and Cortisone Products"; and to the right, "September and the Lack of Harmony of the Autonomous Nerves," between which is inserted the trademark representing a cream-colored Hippocrates surrounded by some Latin aphorism. The red letter in the left corner attracts your glance. The last Sunday in September. The day immediately before when the drowned man in a box is scheduled to be cast up on the outskirts of the seaside park . . . the next day . . . no, it's already today by a few minutes. No matter how you pretend not to see them, the already printed letters do not disappear. It's the same as your chronology written in the past tense. You place your two spread hands separated by shoulder width on the edge of the desk. Yes, that's fine. By shifting your weight forward and supporting yourself on your elbows, you are able to rise easily. Once things are started you cannot stop.

Nevertheless, it's that unfinished affidavit that annoys me. I beg you to destroy it and throw it away before you leave your seat. If things go as planned, such an affidavit will be a useless white elephant, and if they don't, the situation will be a lot worse than the one you describe in it.

AFFIDAVIT—Continued

Now, concerning the incident of the corpse you ask about, I can tell you with certainty that the body is that of the doctor-captain whose names I borrowed in order to practice medicine. The reason why I call him doctor-captain is not because of his old rank but because I used the title for so many years half jokingly and it became a habit with me. Permit me to call him in this way. There was the danger of suicide from sometime past with the doctor, and I am deeply sorry that I was remiss and unable to stop him before anything happened. I regret that very much. I beg you to give me the opportunity of explaining the situation.

The year before the end of the war I was assigned as an orderly to the army doctor in a certain field hospital. Since at the time the doctor was absorbed in his research on producing sugar from wood, I had to take over a good half of the examinations and treatment of patients. Fortunately my memory was good and my hand more than averagely dexterous, and under the guidance of the doctor I was able to perform quite complicated operations. Let me say a word about his research: during the war there was a great shortage of sugar, and sweets were very precious. If he were able to extract sugar from wood, that would be a discovery of world-wide import. The doctor noticed goats eating paper, the raw product of which consisted of wood, and thinking that there must be some active enzyme in the goats' intestines that broke up the cellulose into starch, he devoted himself night and day to separating and extracting it.

One time, I don't know whether it was because he was infected by the goats' intestinal bacteria or whether he was poisoned by tasting the processed wood, the doctor had the misfortune to fall ill. It was a strange sickness: he ran a high fever for three successive days, and after that in three-day cycles he experienced severe muscular cramps accompanied by spasms and nervous disorders. The doctor himself was unable to diagnose his case, and his colleagues gave up on it too. Since then, every time I have the opportunity I watch for literature on the subject, but as yet I have no indication even as to the name of the sickness. As I had long felt kindly disposed toward the doctor, I did my best to care for him. The condition of the sick man seesawed, and there was no satisfactory progress. I still regret to this day that unable to stand the sight of his suffering and in view of his persistent pleading I began to administer drugs to him daily. By the time the war ended, he had already developed symptoms of addiction. However, I did not leave him, and we were demobilized together.·

Even after demobilization, I worked along with the doctor to open a clinic and participated as his assistant in both management and practice. Of course, his illness took no turn for the better, and outside of giving me instructions by means of medical charts the fact was that he was personally incapable of giving examinations or treatment.

Since you ask, I should like to tell you without

covering anything up why I dared to continue to perform illegal medical activities, knowing they were illegal.

First of all there was the necessity of replenishing the doctor's drugs. At this point there was no question of higher or lower rank between us, nor was I at all coerced by him. It was something I did out of a feeling of friendship, spontaneously, and I think that I should hold myself totally responsible. To your question of whether one should not pay special attention to the treatment of drug addicts, I should like to answer in the following way. The treatment of the doctor's drug addiction—he was different from the usual patient—was extremely difficult, and further the actual rate of recovery from addiction is pretty close to zero. While I realize that giving drugs is euthanasia over a period of time, I did not have the courage to abandon him.

Second, I cannot deny the fact that my livelihood was guaranteed under the cloak of the doctor's qualifications. But I did not take advantage of his weak point, his drug habit. The accounting was all in the hands of the doctor's wife, Nana. Only later did Nana and I become intimate, but even so the doctor was afraid that I would abandon him, and he constantly resorted to strong pressure on Nana to establish a relationship with me as a device for keeping me from leaving. This type of persecution complex tends to be frequently observable in the later stages of drug addiction. Third, my realization that daily my reputation was increasing and that my skill was beginning to be recognized was one of the reasons why I dared to continue my practice. Of course, there is no objective measurement by which one can precisely appraise the techniques of a practicing physician. Indeed, I continued, I suppose, because I did not have a strong sense of the crime of charlatanry. What's more, my interest in medicine was gradually growing, and I diligently and ceaselessly absorbed the latest information in medical books and specialized reviews. I considered that twelve years' experience and a conscientious and inquiring mind gave me a confidence in myself that went beyond having or not having a license. In point of fact, I was frequently amazed, when I examined patients that came to me from other hospitals, at the irresponsible and mistaken diagnoses of those doctors who had graduated from the university but who had been poor students there. However, I don't mean to excuse my own offense by that. Whatever my reasons, it is not permissible to infringe the law.

An important turning point occurred in the eighth year. Until then I had got the doctor to take charge of outside contacts such as attending medical meetings; but gradually his abnormal speech and conduct began to be obvious, and abuse and defamation of him, including the suggestion that he was mad, began to get back to us. In addition, since we were being investigated because of the excessive amount of drugs we were using, I also felt in danger; and after talking things over with the doctor we closed the clinic and moved here to this city. That is the course of events up to the present.

But because of this situation, the doctor's mental state grew worse and worse, he became weary of life, and an inclination to suicide became obviously pronounced. At Nana's suggestion we stopped having him appear in public even for outside events and decided that I should register myself as him. Although there were some formal modifications in our setup, the actual situation remained unchanged, even the doctor was in complete agreement with the plan. Fortunately the patients' trust in me was strong here too, and even if my guilt were confirmed I can say that I was confident there would be no damage suits filed nor would I be prosecuted. If we suppose that an injured party that is not aware of being injured is not an injured party, I should like to say that neither was I, who had no sense of having inflicted injury, a person who had caused damage; but for all of that I do not think it is right to break the law. Since I receive protection of life and property as a citizen of the state, it is not possible for me to go against the law.

Now we come down to last year. I have already described how I engaged a new apprentice nurse and how this became the cause of my living apart from Nana. But I report all revenues and expenditures to her and continue to recognize her rights as co-manager. Furthermore, as Nana has recently opened a piano school and is coaching students in the city, after more details on the situation from her I should like to request that you recognize that there are no errors in my statement.

Now no immediate reason occurs to me why the doctor fled the hospital and chose the path of solitary death. He used a room on the second floor; but since he went to bed and got up at varying hours and frequently used the emergency stairs to come and go as he wished, it is impossible to assume responsibility for all his acts. I must tell you of a little dispute that occurred recently. The doctor developed a morbid preference for sweets under the pretext that he missed his old research where he produced sugar from wood. When I tried to curtail his hunger for reasons of his health, he became exceedingly angry. But I cannot believe that that was the cause of his death. Since the corpse was wearing a cardboard box over its head, it is conceivable, I think, that he did not originally intend to die. It is possible he simply slipped during his walk on the embankment still wet from the rain of the day before.

Further, you ask why he was wearing cardboard over his head. I have absolutely no idea. For several months derelicts have been wandering around town wearing cardboard boxes, and there are witnesses too; if you ask whether the cardboard wasn't the doctor's disguise, I cannot go so far as to deny the possibility that he had so dissimulated himself without my knowing it. The doctor seemed to believe that along with his name, address, and license, he had handed me his personality and had become a nobody. Since he also fell into extreme misanthropy, it is not incomprehensible that when he went out he felt like trying to hide himself by wearing a box over his head. As the findings of the autopsy made clear, the scars from the hypodermic needles on the inside of the arm and on the thighs had already formed scabs. When addiction progresses as far as this, it's not worth, I think, being particularly surprised at such eccentric behavior.

There are eyewitnesses who saw a box man enter and leave the hospital; from their testimony and from the scars made by the shots over a long period of time, his connection with the hospital is under suspicion. As a result of that, I have been summoned. Without the eyewitness, the box man would have been disposed of as simply an unidentified body, and I must say, I would find it most regrettable if there were a hint of criticism that I was continuing in my illegal medical practice and not telling anyone. Both the nurse and I had promised not to visit the doctor's room unless he rang for us. Any number of times until now, more than half a day has gone by without our being called. It was only late Sunday night, when we did become suspicious, that we checked the room. I was firmly resolved that if he did not return by dawn, it was absolutely unavoidable to file a search request with the police even though my illegal medical activities would be exposed.

It was the doctor more than anyone else who was strongly against my giving up my medical work. On the one hand, he plied me with flattery and even threatened me with repeated suggestions that if I gave it up he might commit suicide. It's already common knowledge how very cunning and reckless a drug addict is in getting his hands on drugs. Indeed the doctor's suicide would be very troublesome. First, even though I might draw up a death certificate, it would have the same name and surname as mine, and I could scarcely present that to the government office. Repeatedly I had had to entreat the doctor respectfully to put aside the idea of suicide. He, on the contrary, wanted even greater quantities of drugs; his highhanded directions to let him admire the naked body of Toyama Yoko, the newly arrived nurse's apprentice, and to have her give him an enema naked caused me considerable concern. But I didn't necessarily bear him any bitterness. Since those who are sick suffer pain that those in good health do not understand, I consider that they should always be treated with sympathy.

As the doctor had long since come not to need me, I too from now on had no obligation to go on deceiving the world by continuing to engage in illegal medical practice. Illegal medical practice causes trouble for the patient, economically and physically. It was the doctor's view that if there was no claimant there was no crime, but I considered that being a fake doctor did constitute a crime, and I gave a lot of thought to the subject. I should like to use this opportunity of making a clean

breast of everything and put paid to the heavy responsi-
bilities I have borne in my heart for so long.

The above is all true.

The Executioner
Bears No Crime

You have apparently decided at last to take some action. The
vague metallic sound I hear now is that of a syringe being
placed in the sterilizer. I could distinguish that noise alone
from any distance. Like a sand rat that catches the scent of
water over six miles away.

To go on . . . The skylight on the stair landing seems
to be rattling in the wind . . . there's no mistake . . . it is
the sound I can hear only at those times when the door to
your room opens and closes. I can hear . . . the sound of
your bare feet treading cautiously along the corridor of plastic
tile. You are coming slowly along at the rate of about one step
every second. Of course, your head is completely covered by
the box. With the eleventh step the sound changes, and you
seem to be treading on wet mats, and now I imagine you have
just placed your foot on the stair. You are mounting, one step,
and then another, and gradually your pace slows down. Soon
you arrive at the landing and stop for a moment, whereupon
you shift your box half around and look up. Following the
banister along the corridor on the second floor, you come to a
small room at the very end set back the depth of the stairs.
The door is varnished cryptomeria boards, almost indistin-

guishable from the walls and extending the full width of the narrow passage.

Mortuary.

The room is not treated differently because it has dead bodies in it; it is inconspicuous out of consideration for the feelings of patients entering the hospital (or of those who have been there for some time) who are especially sensitive to death. Furthermore the emergency exit is nearby and it is convenient for carrying out the corpses.

Of course, I am not yet a corpse. I am not all that perky, but still I am not a corpse. The reason I who am not dead am in the mortuary—for your sake I should stress this strongly—is not particularly that I am receiving the usual treatment accorded a dead body but that I requested being here. I like this room. That there are no windows more than anything else suits my present mood perfectly. Lately the regulatory function of my pupils seems to have noticeably declined, and daylight makes my eyes tingle as if irritated with sand. Further, I have completely lost human defensive reactions such as feelings of anger, discontent, and hatred and feel very much at home in this room proportioned quite like a coffin . . . the depth being two and a half times the width.

Since you have come to this room you seem motionless. Just as I look for signs of you on the other side of the door, so you too look for signs of me, I suppose. If the door is aware, it is surely having a big laugh over us. However, I understand your feeling of hesitation. No matter how much sympathy you have for me, you must under any circumstances perform the duties of executioner. It is natural that you should be heavy-hearted. Even I, if our places were switched, would tremble and hesitate. Moreover, the one whom you kill is well aware of being killed. You don't look as if you could chatter casually with the one you are cutting up and who is aware of being killed. I wonder if you will feel more at ease if we engage in a debate on death than in small talk. It probably won't work. A debate is even more grotesque. However, as we exchange looks in silence, soon the covering of our nerves will wear thin and produce a short circuit that will burn us badly.

The best thing for you is that I be fast asleep. The best thing is to send me quietly into that other world while I'm asleep. But the light slap of a drug-addicted patient is something you are quite aware of. Though he is drowsy all year long, his sleep is not deep. You are not so foolish as to expect me to sleep soundly. Actually, like this, I'm awake. I am sitting up in bed, and my pen is running right along. I'm wiping away the secretion in my eyes with boric acid, and this is a condition you don't want me in. But you may be at ease. Before your hand touches the handle of the door . . . as soon as you show signs of moving a single pace from there . . . I intend to pretend I am sleeping. You obviously will see through this pretense, I dare say, but you will be more at ease than if I really go to sleep. If I really go to sleep, there is the danger of waking up, but you don't have to worry about that when you feign sleep. Anyway before that I shall drop the notes on the floor and attract your attention and let you know that I am in a consciously feigned sleep. The principal offender in killing me will always be me; you are no more than an accomplice. I have absolutely no intention of pushing the responsibility off onto you alone. Since any time's as good as any other, I want you to begin. Even at this very instant, it makes no difference. The moment you take action will be the end of these notes.

If you wish, I shall leave something like a little posthumous memorandum for you. I think there's no absolute necessity for it, but just by chance it may make you feel better. Yet it's ridiculous to be accused of the crime of helping a suicide.

Here is a town for box men. Anonymity is the
obligation of the inhabitants, and the right to
live there is accorded only to persons
who are no one. All those who are registered are
sentenced by the very fact of being registered.

As with a knitted jacket, everything comes undone from a truly trifling rent. It may be well to cut out the following few lines (seal them up in a vinyl bag so they will not get wet) and fasten them to the fingers of the body. Just a minute. No, not to the fingers but somewhere where it would be easy for the corpse to tie them on himself. Oh yes, what about placing them around the neck in a ring? No, since we want it to appear to be an accidental death, until the investigating authorities, who are suspicious, get here, I should perhaps hide them somewhere in this room. In a pipe coupling of the bed, which will be discovered at once with a little effort, but which at first glance is not obvious. The rest of the notes cut out are, of course, to be incinerated.

> *I personally chose death. If the findings suggest murder, it will all be the fault of my clumsiness. . . .*

No, to make this too apologetic is not wise. Indeed, I may sow the seeds of suspicion if I do. It is better to be more straightforward.

> *I have resolved to die. Let's stop the hypocrisy of hope at this point. Toffee feels pretty hard until you put it in your mouth and suck on it. But you want to crunch it to pieces at once. A piece of candy once broken will never again return to its original form.*

Do I look as if I still have some lingering attachment to life? In spite of myself, my real feelings come out. But worry is useless; no matter how attached I am, attachment is merely that. My reason understands very well that I should not go on living any longer. It's amazing that I should still have my reason. But this reason is as fragile as a castle of sand by the seaside that the rising tide begins to wash over. Another two or three large waves and it will disappear without a trace. At once I change my mind, and greedily I feel like beginning to resist death. First I shall woo the girl boldly, and if I am refused (and refused I shall be), I shall kill her and over a period of days I shall enjoy eating her corpse. This is not a figure of speech; I shall literally put her in my mouth, chew on her, relish her with my tongue. I have already dreamed time and time again of eating her. I won't cook her too much; underdone is fine. She is submissive, and even when she turns into meat, her smile will be unquenchable and she will have a taste somewhere between veal and wild fowl and will be utterly delectable. Apparently my sentiments toward her have been boiled down and now converge into appetite. If my appetite has increased to the point of devouring her, like it or not, I cannot avoid clinging to life. And so, while my reason remains, somehow I wish to wind things up. Of course, suicide is an honorable act, and as long as it is an act, it will not become reality by reason or aspiration alone. A little attachment, a little appetite, become pretexts for hesitation. While my reason is awake, I can manage not to pretend to brush aside at least your helping hand. So I beg of you, won't you please lend me a helping hand while I'm asking for it? It's both for your own good and for mine.

What's wrong? What are you so slow for? I promised that I would pretend I was asleep, didn't I? If you don't hurry it up, I'll turn into a piece of wood or a stone. I suppose you've gone off while I wasn't aware of it. (Probably not. You couldn't be more stealthy than when you came.)

"Are you there? If you are, answer me. What about just coming in?" I tried calling through the door, straining my swollen vocal cords to the utmost.

There was no answer. There was not even any sign of movement. Only the still of night became a pain that was like the striking of an iron plaque, rebounding against my ear-drums. Had I been wrong? I wondered. The sound of the rattling skylight over the stairs and the creaking of the cor-ridor as if a wet mop were wandering along were conceivably due to the suddenly dry wind that came blowing down from the mountains after three days of continuous rain. Further-more, the circumstances were such that I could simply not avoid coming to a hasty conclusion. After all, tonight you did not send her to me. Her naked body should have been an absolute bargaining point for extending my life, for as long as I see her I will not commit suicide. It will soon be ten days since you began preparing the box (my coffin), and since she has not shown her face, there is nothing to do but accept the fact that the preparations are at last completed and the sentence of death has been handed down. Even though the signs beyond the door led me to a hasty conclu-sion, your coming was a matter of time.

After a while the door opens quietly but surely. At once I pre-tend to be asleep. Since there is no one other than you who can open a door so quietly, there is no need to take the trou-ble of checking. I go on feigning sleep. To get used to the stench here, you hold your breath a moment. Before begin-ning to breathe in, you swallow your saliva. A lump of ice as big as a thumb caught in your breast shifts an inch or two lower. You set a plastic water container on the floor and, as you take off the box, look around the long, narrow, windowless room and are again struck by how much it resembles a coffin. For light there is only a single fluorescent thirty-watt tube con-cealed in the ceiling. A sticky ribbon for catching flies, camou-flaged as an artificial rose, is suspended at one extremity of it. In the very middle of the room, immediately below the artifi-cial flower, like a core, is the iron hospital bed. Looking as if I am about to fall out of it, I am asleep like so much gelatine.

With each breath the aftershock makes me quiver like a melted ice pack. My body is like a slice of unsold skate on a fishmonger's counter. The front of the night kimono with vertical stripes is open, and on my stomach, the color of boiled asparagus, is a towel with a flower design faded from too much washing. The two legs that protrude from under the towel show sparse hairs and are moist like freshly skinned squid. Although I try to expel the air I inhale through my nose from my closed mouth, my lips tremble like thick rubber valves. Methane or ammonia crystals cling to the rubber valves and glitter like a dancer's tights. Every time I sleep, my internal organs fall into decay little by little. In speed of decomposition, I would not lose out to any dead body. You hold your nose. Tears come because decomposed substances of oxidized sweat burn your eyes. You can't endure it any longer. Haven't I been saying all along that there's no need to endure? Just think of a murderer as someone who checks the progress of decomposition—and it's true.

You try giving my shoulder a little poke. I continue pretending to be asleep. You wrap a piece of rubber about my upper left arm. With a scalpel you lightly cut the inner side at the elbow and probe for a vein. Since the skin has formed a thick scab, you cannot very well insert a needle directly. The flesh is white and only a little blood comes out. Grasping the vein with absorbent cotton, you thrust in the needle. Darkish blood flows back and is heavy on the inside of the syringe. The plunger is pulled fully out as far as the twentieth notch, but inside there are only three cc's of morphine hydrochloride. You undo the rubber around the upper arm and inject the three cc's. Even if I were to awaken during the process (I cannot awaken since I have been feigning sleep from the beginning), you can think up any number of excuses for vindicating yourself by saying that I am getting morphine only because my breathing is so difficult or some such pretext. In-

stantly my breathing quickens, my relaxed expression becomes even more relaxed, and around my mouth the signs of
death appear. You push the plunger down further. Only air
comes out. The exposed part of my vein dilates like a fish
bladder. You pull out the needle, paint the wound with a
binding agent, and press down hard on it with the flat of your
finger. As there is no need to be concerned about cure or
worry about festering, I shall ignore the rather rough han-
dling. Besides, perhaps I am already deep in a dream. Having
a couple of fingers chopped off would feel just about like
munching on a very peppery Vienna sausage, I should think.
Suddenly my breathing changes drastically again. It becomes
rough and quick, rumbling in my throat like a cat snarling,
and then it cuts off once and for all. In a dream I am standing at the entrance to a city with no shadows; here there are
constructed numberless arches that radiate light. When I rush
through them laughing madly, my body floats gently in the
air. My shadow vanishes and with it my weight. While the I
who is in bed at the time grinds his teeth, the lower half of
my body springs up high (like a fish yanked out of water). It
makes the bed grind its teeth along with me. A thousand
springs, each with a different tone, split open like dry wood
in a bonfire. The grinding merges into the dream, echoes
from one to another among the forest of arches, and begins
to play a funeral dirge for me. As I fly round and round with
my arms clasping my knees, I am terribly cheerful and a little
sentimental. I see a close-up of her sobbing for me. The smell
of winter becomes her, as it does a young larch. When I
stretch out my fingers, a hole opens in the air and becomes an
anus. I am suffocating. When I open my mouth my tongue
flips far out because of the extreme negative pressure on the
outside and will not return to its original position. Just as I
am on the point of inserting my erect tongue into the anus of
air, the dream darkens, comes to a standstill. And I die.

. . .

You come creeping up over the dead me. In your arms you hold the water container. You sit with your buttocks on my chest and your weight causes me to expel my breath. And the end of my breath changes into a sound like the cracking of fish eggs . . . *phut* . . . *phut* . . . After constricting my lungs, you put a large funnel to my mouth and pour in the contents of the tank. At the same time you raise your hips and decrease your weight on me. The tank contains sea water. Little whirlpools dance on the surface of the water in the funnel. The hole gets clogged with scraps of seaweed. When you clear away the refuse, there is a sound like sucking on a decayed tooth, and perhaps the sea water overflows from my mouth. In such a case, it is well to raise your hips more rapidly. When you have fully raised them, the two-quart container is about half empty. With this, preparations for making the body look as if it has met death by drowning are complete.

(Of course, you can't very well deceive the official autopsy. In order to hand down a finding of death by drowning, at the least, sea plankton must be detected in other organs besides the lungs. Sea water contained in the lungs alone would be a very strange trick and would doubtless engender suspicion. And once there was suspicion, in due order my corpse would be a nest of misgivings. There are certain physical signs that cannot be overlooked, no matter how bloated the body is by water or how much the fish have nibbled away at it: the irregular clusters of scars over which corneous tissue has formed stretch along the arm down to the wrist and along the legs to the back of the knees. To anyone it is clear at a glance that this is a drug addict, and what's more one who has been making daily use of drugs for a very long time. If there were a steady underground channel, that would be different, but in a small provincial town like this not many are able to go on procuring supplies of drugs to the point of having so many scars. It might be a terrorist who plays on the weakness of some doctor. Or if not that, the doctor himself. In point of fact, statistically, according to occupation, those who have some relation with medical treatment show the highest rate of becoming addicts. Of course, you are in a bad position, for you have been investigated concerning the amount of drugs used. I think I understand your desire to begin practicing writing an affidavit. But anyway it's too late now. What you can do now is to see to it that the rest goes without a hitch. Come, come, it's all right, everything's sure to be fine. I have just thrown a wet blanket over you, but there's no possibility of a hitch developing now. You must have already reported the existence of vagrants with boxes over their heads to any number of policemen, and the wasteful use of national budgetary funds for legal inquiries concerning dead vagrants, no matter how they die, is prohibited.)

Now the last stage. It is considerable work to carry me down to the bottom of the emergency stairs. I imagine it is really a heavy task for you who are so slight. And then when you lift me to your shoulders, perhaps I puke up some of the sea water from my compressed lungs and get your collar wet. It would be best to take the towel I wear at work and put it around your neck. Then you go back to fetch the box. While you are doing it, don't forget to dispose of the sea water left in the container. A trifling oversight can cause unexpected and fatal results. Then you put the box over my dead body and attach it to my waist with the rope to secure it. This bit of work had best be left until after you load the corpse into the bicycle-drawn trailer. It will also be better to put on the trousers and boots before putting the box on. With that, preparations are all completed. The only thing left to do is to leave. To be on the safe side, don't you think you'd better drape a towel over the top? No, a white towel would only be conspicuous. Furthermore, there's really no danger of running into anyone on the way. Of course, even if you do, you can just get off the road and let them go by. It's downhill all the way, the trailer's axle is well greased, and you should be able to move easily and quietly. But watch out for dogs. You're in trouble if that spoiled mutt follows you. Make sure you chain him up before you set out.

Now as for the place to throw the body, I should like to suggest behind the soy-sauce factory that the two of us decided on before. I can't say that the ground's convenient for hauling a trailer over, but the cliff falls perpendicularly right down to the water, and the fact that anything would most certainly be swept away by the currents makes it an ideal place for throwing a body. While you are doing this, it is already after half past one. At the latest the business will be cleaned up by three. If you don't finish by then, the out-going tide will have passed its peak, the current in the canal will come to a stop, and you won't be able to finish things tonight. If you put off unpleasant things until tomorrow . . .

(*a sudden, unexplained interruption*)

Another Insertion . . .
the Last

Well, now, the time seems to have come to clarify the real situation. I intend to take off the box, reveal my face, and let you and only you know just who the real author of these notes is and just what his real objective has been.

Perhaps you will not be able to believe me, but there is absolutely no falsehood in what I have written. Products of imagination perhaps, but no falsehoods. A falsehood deceives and makes one stray from the truth, but imagination can be a short cut leading one rather to the truth. We have already got to within a pace of it. Everything will suddenly become clear with a last little correction.

Of course, I am under no obligation to confess the truth. In the same way you are under no obligation to believe it either. This is not a matter of obligation but clearly one of actual advantage or disadvantage. There is no advantage in deception. I don't want to talk about some detective story that can have a variety of solutions.

Of course, I feel that lately the signs of the times are more and more going in a direction unsuitable to detective stories. As I write this, the way in which the installment-plan system is expanding, for example, occurs to me. Just as there are almost no more people who are afraid of shots, contrary to times past, now there are few who shrink from installment buying. But with installment buying one mortgages everything, one exposes oneself, one's work, one's house to securing the money borrowed. Almost everyone has a good name and a reliable profession to be able to obtain clearance, and quite naturally roles for criminals and detectives are very few. These days only a guerrilla or a box man would want to cover up his identity to the extent of refusing the convenience of installment buying. But I am that box man. A representative of anti-installment-ism. Even if I am against the times, I should like to end with a clear solution: the denouement of these notes.

Now I wonder just what you think about euthanasia. For your information I shall cite the official precedent handed down by the Nagoya Superior Court in February, 1955.

EUTHANASIA IS PRACTICABLE UNDER THE FOLLOWING CONDITIONS:

1 When a sick person has contracted an incurable disease and is threatened by imminent death;
2 When the pain experienced is obviously unbearable;
3 When the object is the elimination of the sick man's pain;
4 When the person in question is fully lucid, gives his consent, and specifically requests euthanasia.
5 If there is ample reason for approving such a step, any medical intervention is to be performed by a physician.
6 The means of causing death should be morally appropriate.

In my own opinion the text of this legal precedent clings somewhat too much to physical dimensions. From the standpoint of human interpretation, I think it is too timid, too conventional. Sometimes there are cases where sickness of the mind and the suffering of the body are equally appalling. But at this point such matters are unimportant.

What I wanted to say is just that if one has to do with people who live where the law does not apply, then all murders there are euthanasia. The murder of a box man cannot be a crime any more than killing on a battlefield or punishment meted out by an executioner. For the sake of experimentation, try applying to a box man the clause about the sick man in the above legal precedent. I'm sure you understand that like the enemy soldier or the condemned criminal the box man too leads an existence in which, legally, from the beginning, his very survival is not recognized.

Thus rather than asking who is a real box man, it would be better to ascertain who is not a real one; that is an easier approach to reality, I think. A box man has experiences that only a box man can talk about, adventures that apply to him alone, that a fake box man can never tell.

For example, the first several summer days a box man experiences on becoming a box man are the beginning of his ordeals. A feeling of suffocation makes him want to scratch out his memories with his nails. But if it's only the heat, one feels one can somehow still put up with it. If worst comes to worst, one can go to the entrance to a building facing an underground passage and get the outflow of the air conditioning. The uncomfortable thing is the sticky sweat that has no time to dry and builds up layers of dirt. They constitute only too good a culture for bacteria, yeast, and mold. Below the layers of fermented dirt the sweat glands stop breathing, panting and gasping like dried mollusks at low tide. The itching of disintegrating skin is more difficult to stand than any visceral pain. Stories of torture where one is covered with tar or where some dancing girl painted with gold dust goes insane are very meaningful to me. The whiteness of fruit from which the skin has been peeled away with a knife flickers radiantly before my eyes. So many times I have thought how I would like to strip off my own skin including the box the way one peels off the skin of a fig.

But in the long run, my attachment to the box won out. After four or five days, perhaps my skin had become used to the dirt, but I experienced almost no discomfort. Or perhaps my body, as far as the skin's rate of breathing was concerned, had adapted itself to husbanding the amount of oxygen consumption. If that were true, then I who had originally sweated profusely at this summer's end had come to sweat but very little. As long as one sweats he is a fake box man.

While I am about it, let me write about the Wappen beggars. That's the most unpleasant person a box man can meet. Doting old beggars all covered with insignia and badges and toy decorations like fish scales, with little flags bearing the rising sun sticking out of their caps like birthday-cake candles. One came after me shrieking every time he saw me. Once I was unable to avoid his surprise attack, for being used to ignoring him, and was inadvertently off my guard. Emitting senseless shrieks, he swept down on me and thrust something in from above the box. Later, when with difficulty I had driven the beggar away and drawn the object out, I saw that it was a little flag with a rising sun that had graced his cap.

I was profoundly disturbed. Another few inches to the side, and the haft might have pierced my ear. After that, with Wappen beggars only, I decided to strike first, though I don't usually. Thanks to that I have been able to get the hang of throwing heavy things from the box. In the first place (in case one is right-handed), horizontally on the inside you bend your right arm, that goes out through the observation window, using the elbow as a fulcrum and twisting the upper part of your body including the box to the left. Following your body back, you extend your arm firmly in the direction of the objective. Essentially it's a discus throw without the running. You can't claim to be a real box man unless you can deal with Wappen beggars.

But usually a box man's days, after he goes out into town, pass tranquilly. There are almost no incidents that merit the name. One's self-consciousness and diffidence toward others at most last only two or three months. Clinging to one's outward appearance interferes with living. No matter how much one may be a box man, he cannot very well stop such daily functions as eating, defecating, and sleeping. For sleeping and evacuation, one doesn't choose any special place, but that will hardly do for eating. When the foodstuffs on hand are exhausted, like it or not, one can't very well not bestir oneself. If you want to get food without paying and without causing trouble, the first thing is to go foraging for leftovers. And for that you naturally turn in the direction of the busier areas of the city that have both abundance and variety.

Foraging for food has its own knack to it. But the situation is different from that of vagrants and beggars, who have gradually got used to the circumstances of foraging; not anything will do for a box man just because it is edible. It's not a question of luxury but of a sense of hygiene. It doesn't necessarily follow that leftovers are unclean, but one way or another the impression they make is not very pleasing. One is especially disconcerted by the foul odors. Over a period of three years, in the final analysis, the stench was the only thing I was never able to accustom myself to.

I remained unaccustomed to the smell because of the disagreeable feeling produced by tastes that did not match. Fish have the smell of fish, meat that of meat, vegetables that of vegetables—everything has its own individual smell, and when we confirm the quantities as they mix together in our mouths, we are at ease and satisfied. If we expect fried shrimp, we are nonplused at the taste of bananas. A piece of chocolate is disgusting if it has the taste of fried clams. All the more then, there is no way of equating a given food to the smells of leftovers that are mixed together at random. Even if one understands this situation in principle, psychologically it is quite unacceptable.

Now the first step in foraging for food is to look for those items which as much as possible are dried and odorless. However, these are surprisingly troublesome. Leftovers thrown out by restaurants generally fall into two categories. The first are those goods that easily deteriorate, that do not keep well; and from the standpoint of quantity these are overwhelmingly the most numerous. Inedibles (used chopsticks, wastepaper, broken dishes, and the like) are placed apart, and the edibles are gathered in great plastic containers, which are picked up by the trucks from the hog farms every morning. The second category comprises those items that have a definite shape and cannot be served again to one client after the preceding one has left—for example, bread, fried items, dried fish, cheese, pastry, fruit, and the like. They would seem to be common enough, but no matter how you hunt you cannot find them. I wonder if it's because they can be used again since they do not rot easily even though they are divided into pieces. Indeed, if you break up dried bread you get breadcrumbs, and you get delicious stock from plain fried fish and chicken bones.

I'm sure I wrote about this before, but a box man can easily obtain food from store counters. He doesn't actually need to resort to foraging for leftovers. But it does provide a good opportunity to get accustomed to the town which you really have to do in order to enjoy life as a box man among the crowds. When he's used to the town, wherever he is, time begins to describe concentric circles around the box man as the center.

The false goals of those
Who have kept running, but
Who have never caught up—
The night stadium . . .
Where the flag still flies
But that both umpire and spectator
Have long since forsaken.

One is absolutely never bored, for the background goes by swiftly; but the foreground passes at a snail's pace, and at the center things are perfectly still. Anyway it's the fake box man who's bored in his box.

Now I'd like to have you think about this. Which one of us was not a box man? Who failed to become a box man?

The Case of D

D was a boy who yearned to be strong. Often he would pray to be stronger. But he didn't know how to increase his strength Suddenly it occurred to him one day: he decided to try and construct a kind of periscope out of plywood and cardboard and mirrors. At either end of a tube he placed two parallel mirrors inclined at an angle of forty-five degrees, by which his eye shifted to the further extremity of the tube held horizontally or vertically. He attached paper hinges especially to the mirror situated at the upper end, and by manipulating a cord from below he had a device where the angle could be altered considerably.

For the first test, he decided to try it out between the fence and shed of a neighborhood apartment. It was a place that he had discovered as a child when he still used to play hide-and-seek; a narrow space set at a blind angle with the street and, of course, the side of the apartment. When he crouched down he could smell the odor of mouse droppings mixed with the smell of wet earth. First, supporting his two arms on his knees, he pressed the body of the peri-scope firmly to his forehead. Gradually he tried pushing the upper end above the fence. The street was a steep slope, and even the pedestrians who were quite tall did not come to the height of the wall there. Furthermore, since the footing on the slope was not very secure, very few people paid any attention to anything above eye level. Reassuring himself, D calmed his fears, but when he saw the vista of the street reflected in the mirror in which he was looking, he was terror-stricken. He had the impression that the whole view had turned into eyes that reproached him. Instinctively he ducked his head. As he did so the tip of his periscope struck against the fence and simply broke off with a wet thud like the squashing of an orange. He repaired it with cellophane tape as he wiped away the sweat that pearled on his face.

The second time he continued watching in defiance of the vista that bore down on him from the eyepiece. When he once tried returning the pressure, his tension too simply began to slacken. When he realized that there was no reason to fear anyone's looking back at him, his sense of guilt vanished at once, and the vista began to change before his eyes. He was vividly aware of the change in the relationship between himself and the scene, between himself and the world. It would appear·that he had not indeed missed his first objective in constructing the periscope.

There was nothing particularly novel. Every detail of the scene was pervaded by a soft but penetrating light, and everything that struck the eye was velvety smooth and graceful. Anything that might cause feelings of hostility was completely erased from the pedestrians' expressions and from their actions. Nowhere was there a cross or faultfinding glance to be seen. The rough edges had been taken from the various projections and depressions that made up the view—street signs, telephone poles, walls, and concrete pavement. The world was filled with a softness as of an early Saturday evening that would go on forever. He looked playfully at the street beyond the mirror. And the street returned the smile of the amorous boy. Just by looking at it, the world was happy for him. In his imagination he put his signature to a peace treaty between himself and the world.

Thoroughly encouraged, D, who had become courageous, peered at the street, shifting from place to place. The street too did not challenge him. As long as he looked through the periscope, the world was unconditionally magnanimous. One day he artfully thought up a little adventure. He decided he would try peeking at the toilet of the place next door. It was an independent cottage a little way from the main house inhabited by a lady instructor in gymnastics at the Middle School. Perhaps she did not actually live in the cottage but, simply taking advantage of the fact that it was soundproofed, from time to time played the piano there. He was not very clear about that, nor did he particularly try to find out.

But once the thought of spying on her occurred to him, he had the feeling that he had been thinking of it for a long time. He even felt that all his efforts had been in preparation for that. The cottage came flush to the fence and directly on the other side of it was his little study that had been made independent by partitioning off the end of a corridor. Thanks to this position, the sounds of flushing water in the toilet were clearly far more audible, far nearer, than the muffled voice of the piano, whose high notes were deadened by the soundproofed walls. As a matter of fact the sound of the piano and the noise of flushing were not audible at the same time, but in D's head the lady teacher's favorite piece, which was sweet and sad and which she always played last in her practicing, and the sound of rushing water mixed with the swirling air in the white porcelain cavity overlapped in a seemingly meaningful way. At the mere thought of a human presence in the neighboring toilet he had the impression of smelling steaming urine, and the accustomed melody was enough to make the sinews of his back twitch with sensual desire.

According to reconnaissance that he had previously carried out on the sly, there was a narrow opening for sweeping out the dust at just about floor level. If that were open, there would be no problem; but if not, the only thing left was to peek in through the vent near the ceiling. It would be difficult to see through, but it would be absolutely reliable since there was only an insect screen, for the ventilating fan had been removed (it was doubtless out of order). But as much as possible he liked to peek into toilets from below. By simply imagining the act of peeking, a squirming living cream fell into his eyes.

According to his reckoning up until now, the lady teacher next door finished practicing the piano sometimes about five o'clock in the afternoon and other times about eight. The probabilities of her going to the bathroom after practicing were greater around eight o'clock. But as far as he was concerned that time was inconvenient. Since both his parents were at home, it was difficult to go out into the garden. At five o'clock his father would not yet have returned home, and his mother was liable to be out doing the shopping for the evening meal. If he was going to carry out his plan, five o'clock was decidedly the time. As it was still light, there was the danger of being discovered by the teacher, but then he could only have faith in the periscope. By observing the town from various places, he had gained absolute confidence in managing the instrument. Furthermore, once he had made up his mind, the impulse to peek covered his hesitation like a thick coat of primary color.

When he got back from school that day, in order to ensure his freedom around five o'clock, he made up some excuse to delay his mother's shopping. About four forty, after he had made sure that the practicing was over and that the usual final piece had begun, he at last got his mother out. After slipping on a pair of canvas gym shoes with the backs trodden down, and with his periscope under his arm, he sneaked out into the garden. Contrary to what he had imagined, the periscope would not reach the little window from this side of the board fence. Being caught in the act of peeking on *this* side of the fence might be rather more sticky. He felt that the chances of being challenged would be less by getting on the other side. As long as he didn't expressly inform his victim that he was peeking . . . as long as his victim, even if she was aware that she was being spied on, kept on pretending to take no notice . . . he vaguely expected that a kind of collusion would arise between the person being spied on and the person spying. He certainly could not consider that the timid and reserved confession of love that peeking is was all that censurable.

D slipped under the board fence and came up on the other side. It was more damp than the garden of his own house. The space between the building and the fence was scarcely two feet wide, and it was rare that anyone entered; spongy liverwort formed a thick covering. Slipping in sideways, he crouched in the space between the toilet and the fence. He was lucky. The edge of the dust opening was open about two inches. Naturally he used the periscope horizontally. His breathing quickened and his chest hurt. Leaning back against the fence, he closed his eyes. After taking a breath, he adjusted the periscope and took his position. First of all, the porcelain toilet bowl came into view. It was not white as he had imagined it, but a baby blue. Yet the floor was of white tiles, and rubber sandals painted silver stood in a line. No matter how he adjusted the mirrors, the field of vision just shifted right and left and he was not able to establish the necessary angle. He must be calm. Since he was using the instrument horizontally, he would have to revolve the tube so as to see up and down. The walls were plyboard printed with wood grain.

It seemed to him that time passed extremely slowly. The music too today seemed especially long. His whole body felt warm, and his breathing sounded like a whistle. His cranium opened with the pressure, and his eyeballs flew out like cork bullets. His mother would doubtless be coming back soon. The pretentious rhythms of the piano attacked the joints of his knees like some nervous disease. He was carried away by a compulsion to enter the house, to destroy the piano.

Nevertheless, the music somehow drew to an end. Soon came the several final bars he was accustomed to . . . then the final drawn-out chord. D told himself not to expect too much, that to anticipate success the first time would be too presumptuous. Since the temperature today was high and the day dry, the number of times one urinated would necessarily be proportionately fewer. Yet, he could not but be expectant. D began to quiver. He could not get enough air through his nose alone. He left his mouth open, and his whole body was pulsating like a pump.

Suddenly a voice sounded next to his ear.

"And just who are you? What are you doing? And don't try and get away. If you do I'll report you."

He cringed. He was pinned to the ground. He had no strength to shift his glance in order to see from what direction the voice was coming. His gasping breathing, he thought, was like the red, lighted end of a sparkler dangling at the end of its paper string.

"Go around in front and come in through the entrance." The voice was not all that threatening, and that was a relief. "All right . . . get up . . . quickly now." Quite definitely the voice seemed to come from the toilet. But he could see no one. From where and how, he wondered, could he be seen? "Don't forget that weird piece of machinery there. Go directly round in front. The door's not locked, and you can come right in." Was she going to finish urinating, he wondered, or would she stop now? The position of his periscope was definitely wrong. "Do you understand? You're not to run away. Now go around in front right away, and no loitering."

It looked as if there were nothing for him to do except do as he was told. It certainly seemed out of the question to take to his heels. If he interpreted the warning not to run away as meaning that if he did not she would not report him to the school or to his parents, then whatever his punishment he had best get it over with here. In the state of mind of a lamb being led to slaughter and clutching his periscope that had proved useless to his breast, he circled the building and proceeded in the direction of the entrance. The door, which had always suggested to him the sensation of touching folds of flesh, had now changed to a feeling of concrete.

Immediately inside the door was a spacious music room with a piano. He saw the sound-absorbent wood dotted with holes that gave him an itchy sensation just looking at it. On the floor lay a green carpet. At the same time as he closed the door behind him another inner door opened, and the lady instructor entered. Behind her came the sound of flushing water. She had evidently finished urinating after he had been discovered. In a corner of his conscience her white buttocks projecting into the toilet bowl overlapped with the swirl of the flushing. Since he could not raise his face he experienced an oppression as if he were face to face with her naked buttocks.

"I'll lock the door," she said, going around in back of him, and there was the sound of a key turning over.

"You're not ashamed, are you?"

"Yes, I am."

"Your voice is beginning to change. What you did is natural, I suppose, but I hate dirty acts. You are probably ashamed, but I am a lot more. To the extent you're embarrassed you make me feel embarrassed too. What are we to do? If I gloss it over, you'll just repeat the same thing. . . ."

"No, I won't."

"I wonder."

"I really won't."

"But even so, I can't very well let you go completely unpunished, can I. I think it would be best to make you experience the same feelings that you caused me."

The lady teacher turned to the piano and suddenly began to let her fingers run over the keyboard. It was a section of the piece she habitually played last of all. It was splendid, like piled marbles, quite different from the sound audible through the wall. It was like a silken flag softly streaming in the breeze. Increasingly D thought himself wretched and dirty, and finally he was unable to stop the overflow of tears.

"What do you think of this piece?"

"Oh, I like it."

"Do you really?"

"I like it very much."

"Do you know who the composer was?"

"No."

"It was Chopin. Wonderful, marvelous Chopin." Suddenly she stopped playing the piano and stood up. "Well, then, take off your clothes. Strip naked. I'll go in the other room."

D did not at once take in what she had said. Even when the lady teacher had withdrawn, he simply remained standing absently for some time.

"What's wrong? Why are you so slow?" came her voice from the other side of the door. "I'm looking at you right

now through the keyhole. If you really think you embarrassed me, you can surely do what I ask."

"What am I supposed to do?"

"But I told you! Take off your clothes. Since you put
me in exactly the same position, no excuses now."

"Won't you forgive me?"

"Certainly not. Would it be better if I reported it to
your father or your mother?"

D was defeated. His stomach sank to his bladder, and
his chest seemed to become hollow. He didn't particularly
dislike getting naked. Concerning that point, in his own
way he assumed that they would come to a mutual understanding. But he was not at all self-confident. If he were to
strip, like it or not, he was sure to get an erection. Would
the lady instructor ever pardon his reacting like that? he
wondered. It was unbelievable that she would. She would
get angry and this time would certainly not overlook his
offense. Or if not that, she would hold her sides with laughter. Whichever, he was too miserable. Since he realized that
he was so wretched, he wondered if his erection would not
go down a bit. But it wouldn't work. Just by thinking of
being naked he had already started to get a hard-on. Even
while he was being laughed at, his erection would keep on
growing.

He resigned himself. Braving his own ugliness, he took
off his coat, stripped away his shirt, and lowering his trousers,
he was stark naked. He was firmly erect. Yet there was no
reaction. Beyond the door everything remained perfectly
quiet. It was not simply that there was no sound, but a hush
like some substance was cowering there. Her gaze, turning
into black light, came piercing through the keyhole. From
his field of vision the color vanished and there was only
chiaroscuro. Sensation vanished from the soles of his feet.

As he tottered along he began to pass water. It was not urine, but a seminal emission. He could not stop himself once he had started. He fell on his knees, and covering his face with his hands, he pretended to cry. There were, of course, no tears. In an instant his viscera dried up like a beach at dawn.

"Do you understand now?" Her voice on the other side of the door was dry too. He nodded. Indeed, he understood very well. He understood profoundly, more than his nod to her indicated, more than he himself realized.

"You had better go home now."

The inner door opened a crack, and the key to the front door that came flying in fell soundlessly to the floor. It was a door he could have opened without a key from the inside.

. . .

The door of the hospital that I finally reached is locked, and a card announcing that there are no examinations today has been hung out. In the back the friendly dog sniffs hoarsely through its nose. I ring the bell. Being impatient, I push on it without letting up. There is an indication that someone is coming. Suddenly the door is flung open, and the girl with wide-open arms hastily invites me in. She walks away toward the inside as she says something quickly. I do not really catch what she says, but apparently she is grumbling to herself, mistaking me for the fake box man (or the fake doctor). The best thing is to correct this sort of misapprehension at once. Coughing, I begin to explain.

"I'm not the doctor. I'm the real thing . . . the genuine article. The former photographer who was waiting under the bridge last night. . . ."

With parted lips she quickly scrutinizes me from top to toe. Her expression is vague with surprise.

"I'm in a quandary," she says. "You didn't keep your promise, did you. Take off your box right away. Maybe you don't know it, but . . ."

"Oh, yes, I do. You're talking about the doctor. I saw him a little while ago in the street."

"Take it off . . . please."

"But I can't. That's why I came running in such a hurry."

"That won't work . . . not at the point we're at."

"But I'm naked. Stark naked. After I saw you at the hospital I took a shower at the bathhouse and was waiting for the underclothes I washed to dry. I've got to put something on before I can leave the box. I planned to come here after disposing of it. Because I want you to see how I keep my promises. But I fell asleep. I slept so hard it was like being rolled over and crushed under a construction roller. Furthermore, I had a series of dreams, and since I could not sleep in them, although I remained lying down until a while ago, I'm still suffering from lack of sleep. But when I opened my eyes, my underclothes and trousers that had been hung out to dry had vanished. What a mess! I had the impression that near dawn I had had a dream in which a lot of children raced around with a flag attached to the end of a pole, but perhaps it wasn't a dream but actually happened. When I thought about it I had the feeling that it wasn't a flag but my trousers. I didn't know what to do. Somewhere, somehow, I had to get at least some trousers. I would find some trousers, any old rags would do. As I thought about it, I headed in the direction of the town, whereupon a box man, exactly the same as I, was walking in the area at the end of the embankment. Too late, I thought. I had no time for trousers. I had to get to the hospital."

Suddenly she begins to laugh. Supporting her body bent double on her heels, she shakes with laughter. At first the laughter is unpleasant and jeering; but in the midst of it the sting leaves it, and it turns into amused laughter. She finishes laughing, relaxed, and her tone changes to a cheerful and friendly one.

"I don't mind if you're naked. A promise is a promise."

"I'm sorry. Can't you lend me some trousers? Any old ones will do."

"Well, then, I'll strip too. Anyway you mean to take my picture, I imagine. We don't have to be shy, do we, with both of us naked?"

"There's not much point in seeing a man naked, is there?"

"Oh, you're wrong," she replies expressionlessly, beginning at once to take off her clothes. Blouse . . . skirt . . . brassière. "I don't like that box. I can't stand it another second."

She stands without reserve before me naked. About her lips there is a touch of teasing. But in her eyes lurks dark entreaty. She is naked, but she doesn't seem to be at all. Being naked suits her too well. But that is not true of me. The lower half of my body, particularly, that peeks out from the box is exceedingly comical, I imagine. "Close your eyes a while. Turn in that direction."

"All right," she says, her voice filled with laughter, and turning her back, she leans her shoulder against the wall of the corridor. As I take off my boots, I have the feeling that my whole body is shaking slightly. Quietly I extricate myself from the box, noiselessly approach her from behind, and put a hand on her shoulder. As she does not try to resist, I reduce the distance between us even more. I tell myself emphatically as I do so that I must forever maintain this closeness.

"Is it all right? What if the doctor should come back?"
"He won't. He doesn't even want to . . ."
"The smell of your hair is so good."
"What a beautiful, firm ass . . ."
"I confess . . . I was a fake."
"Ssh . . . don't say any more. . . ."
"But these notes are the real thing. They're the will the real box man gave me to keep."
"You're all sweaty. . . ."

> (But there's no need to apologize. Writings left
> behind by the dead can't always be taken at face
> value as inevitably relating the truth. Those who
> are going to die have jealousies and envies that are
> incomprehensible to those who remain. Among
> them are those perverse ones whose hatred for the
> empty promises of "truth" cuts to the bone and
> who at best nail the coffin lid on with lies. One
> can't very well swallow the bait whole by just
> claiming it is the writing of the dead.)

In His Dream the Box Man Takes His Box Off. Is This the Dream He Had Before He Began Living in a Box or Is It the Dream of His Life After He Left It . . . ?

My destination was the house located at the top of a slope at the exit from the city. After having traveled far and wide in a horse-drawn carriage I have finally just arrived before the city gate. Judging from the length of my voyage, the house is probably at the entrance rather than at the exit of the town.

Furthermore, the horse-drawn carriage is only a manner of speaking, for the vehicle was drawn not by a horse but in fact by a man wearing a cardboard box over his head. More precisely it was my father. Father was already over sixty. Naturally he had certain conservative aspects, and since he wholeheartedly refused to break the custom handed down from ancient times in the village that at a wedding the bride must be met with a horse-drawn carriage, he himself had gone out to do so, taking the place of the horse. However, so as not to cause me embarrassment he had hidden himself in a cardboard box. It was also out of consideration for the bride lest he shock her.

Of course, if I had just had the money to hire a horse-drawn carriage, my father would never had had to go to such extremes, nor would I ever have asked him. However, it would be simply too bad to give up the wedding because I could not pay the fee for the carriage. Indeed, I could only depend on my father's good offices.

But my already sixty-year-old father was not after all a horse. Since he was panting up a rough, sloping road, his progress was not one tenth that of a real horse. Nor could I very well get down and push from behind; the carriage crept slowly along. Time alone went wildly by. Furthermore, with the merciless jolting there was no reason for me to be blamed if the demands of nature finally reached their limit.

The carriage stopped. Father undid from the box something that looked like a leather belt (I don't know its name) that attached to the horse's belly and, looking up at me from the open observation window in the front of the box, smiled weakly a wan, exhausted smile. I smiled back at him stiffly, and slowly crawled down from the baggage cart. I said a carriage, but actually it was a baggage cart. There was no agreement that it shouldn't be a baggage cart, and after I got married I could do with it what I wanted. Breathing hard, I ran shufflingly to the side of the road, at the same time opening my fly. As the pressure drained from my belly I experienced in a profound feeling of liberation as if I were flying away over some distant range of mountains.

"Chopin! What a thing to do!"

From behind me came Father's perplexed cry. I had been too careless. Between the bride's house and the road stood a great thicket of palms, and I was sure that I was completely screened off by them. But my bride had tired of waiting. Apparently she had caught the sound of the carriage from a distance and had come out right to the roadside to welcome me. Out of timidity and constraint she had concealed herself, ironically, right behind the palms that served as a shield for me. Our gazes crossed. It was certain that she saw my penis. Her white garment fluttered between the branches, and I could hear her light, running steps and the sound of a door being slammed as with a wooden mallet. Everything was lost. As I crossed over the wavering rope stretched between hope and despair, my breast aflame, and as I was about to reach the opposite side in just one more step, the ax had fallen. I was profoundly disappointed.

"You're her guardian, Father. Do something, I beg you."

Tears of resentment came welling up. As I sobbed compulsively, my urine still kept flowing. It dug a hole in the ground and formed a light yellow pond that gave off steam as it spread out.

"Listen, Chopin, it's best you give the whole thing up," reasoned my father sympathetically as he tapped in a staccato on the belly of the box with a hand that he had stuck out through the hole. "You had better stop this useless struggling. A man who's got a mania for indecent exposure is not suited to marriage . . . it's common sense . . . to young girls today."

"But I don't have any mania for indecent exposure!"

"It probably seems so to her. You were seen, you know."

"But we're going to be married anyway, so what difference . . ."

"Out of consideration for your father who has gone as far as to take the place of a horse, couldn't you bow out like a man? I beg of you. Fortunately there were no other eyewitnesses. No matter how many hundreds of volumes of Chopin's biography may be written, I won't want anyone to know of this scandal. A fate governed by urinating is not at all suitable for a biography. Really not at all. Of course, I don't say you're at fault. Responsibility should be placed on the prejudice about indecent exposure and on the municipal administration that neglects the construction of public toilets. Well, let's get going. You don't have any attachment to this town. Let's go to a big city where there are a lot of public johns. If only we could find a public toilet, we could urinate and defecate to our heart's content."

The wound to my heart would not be cured by going to a city. But why did my father refer to me as Chopin? Thinking that I was not the only one who was hurt, I decided not to persist. Hold on . . . I quite agreed with Father when he said that this town was no longer any place to stay. My defenselessness as I stood urinating made me feel keenly uneasy.

We abandoned the carriage. But my father flatly refused to take off the box. As the responsibility for the present situation was half his, he insisted that it was his duty as my father to go on playing the role of the horse for the time being. Thereupon I got astride my father's box and turned my back on the town I had lived in for so long.

When we arrived in the city we at once took a garret room with a piano and decided to put our time to good use. I had the impression that we had simply turned and entered her house from the back, but that point was not clear. Handwork is best for diverting attention from grief. Father got hold of some art paper and pens somewhere or other. Using the piano as my desk, I devoted myself to drawing her from memory. Needless to say, as I became more practiced, the portraits turned into those of a nude woman.

"Chopin, your talent's not bad. I admit that, and I think you realize it, but then our financial situation is not so terribly brilliant. So how about it? Try to go easy on the paper and paint smaller pictures."

Father was right. But whether the paper was large or small was not the point. It was easier to draw smaller pen sketches. I continued working, gradually decreasing the size of the paper. Since I was proportionately more rapid finishing a drawing when I reduced the dimensions, I used more and more paper. At length, using a magnifying glass and attaching pieces of paper the size of the flat of my thumb with pins to my board, I accustomed myself to drawing lines so fine that they were indistinguishable to the naked eye. Only during the time I concentrated on this work could I be with her.

At one point I noticed something strange. The garret room, which should have been perfectly quiet, was filled with people. Why had I not noticed until now? From the door to the front of the piano a queue had formed and apparently stretched out into the corridor. The person at the head put money into the box (my father, of course) beside the piano and received with great deference the picture I had just finished painting. I was not all that taken aback. I also sensed that this situation had been going on for quite some time. That is, the food had got much better lately, and the old piano that served as a desk had at one point transformed into a new grand. Father's box as well had made great progress; from cardboard it had turned into one of genuine red leather with buckles. All unbeknownst to me we were apparently beginning to be widely accepted by the world. No sooner did I make a picture than it was sold, and no matter how many I went on sketching, the line of buyers showed absolutely no signs of slackening.

But at this point such a state of affairs was without importance. Apparently with the money we earned we had bought a real horse, but that had nothing to do with me. Actually, since the breakup of the marriage I had never seen my father once leave the box, and so I was in fact suspicious whether he was my real father or not. My dejection came from the fact that although the girl in my pictures was always the same, the real girl had grown older with the passage of time, and I should never be able to get her back. Every time I thought about it, the pain of our parting was vividly re-

vived, and from my slackened tear ducts tears began to overflow for no reason at all. Instantly, my father stretched his
hand from the box, shook out a new silk handkerchief, and
applied it to my eyes. Anyway since the picture I was drawing
was small, it would smudge at once with a single teardrop and
be useless.

Since I have been painting these pictures there is no
person who does not know my name now. You won't see an
encyclopedia that doesn't have an article on Chopin as the
producer as well as the inventor of the first stamp in the
world. But mail operations have progressed, and along with
their gradual nationalization my name has become known
as that of a counterfeiter of stamps. This is apparently
the most convincing reason why my portrait cannot be ex-
hibited in any post office. Only the red of the red box that
my father regularly used at the end of his life is even now,
in part, used on postboxes.

Five Minutes
to Curtain Time

—A sultry wind is blowing between you and me now. A
sensual, burning wind is blowing around us. I do not know
precisely when it began. In the force of the wind and in the
heat I seem to have lost my sense of time.

But in any case I realize too that the direction of the
wind will probably change. Suddenly it will turn into a cool
westerly wind. And then this hot wind will be stripped away
from my skin like a mirage, and I shall not even be able to

recollect it. Yes, the hot wind is too violent. Within itself is concealed the premonition of its end.

Why, I wonder? If I search for the explanation it will not be impossible to find. Yet the important thing is whether or not you intend to listen to it. Anyway I realize that I'm putting on a one-man show, but I don't want to bore you. What about it . . . shall I go on, or . . . ?

—Yes, yes, if you make it short. . . .

—Short? About five minutes . . . ?

—Five minutes will be just about right, I think.

—Of course, we're in love, you know. It's a different love from one that gradually grows, turning into a soaring tower of mist, solidifying, and reaching completion. It's a paradoxical love, beginning at the end . . . a love that commences from the realization that it is lost. A poet said it well. It is beautiful to love, but ugly to be loved. In love that begins with lost love, therefore, there are no shadows at all. I do not know whether it is beautiful or not, but in any case there is no grief in the pain of this kind of love.

—Why is that?

—Why is what?

—What's the purpose of going on talking about what's over and done?

—It's not over. Our affair begins with love lost. Actually the fiery wind is blowing harder.

—It's because it's summer that it's hot.

—Apparently you're incapable of understanding. This is a tale, of course. This story is in the act of taking place. Since you hear it you have the obligation of being one of the cast of characters. Now you're told someone's in love with you. What a quandary I'll be in if you don't play the part you're assigned, no matter how uncomfortable or ridiculous.

—Why, I wonder?

—The important thing is not the end. The thing to consider is the reality of your feeling the fiery wind on your skin. The denouement is not the problem. Now the fiery wind itself is important. In this fiery wind words and sensations that have been asleep give out a blue light as if they possess high-voltage electricity. This is a rare time when a man can see with his eyes the soul as substance.

—Amazing. If you woo one like that you'll manage never to be hurt. But your intentions are too obvious.

—I suppose . . . about half is true. But if you can't accept the other half at all, we might as well stop.

—You do want to go on don't you?

—Of course.

—You have the right to two minutes more.

—You're forcing yourself.

—You had better not waste any time.

—All right, I'll be careful of the time. I don't expect to get time back. Compared to the you in my heart, the I in yours is insignificant. But when I try to escape from that pain time melts slowly away. If I seriously command the techniques of wooing, then there is hope of coming into possession of a little peace and happiness. So I want to cherish that fiery wind that is so difficult to come by, that begins with love lost. Marvelous forests of words and seas of desire . . . time stops just by touching your skin lightly with my fingers, and eternity draws near. In the pain of this fiery wind a physical transformation that will not disappear until I die is effected on me.

Whereupon the Play Came to an End Without Even the Bell Ringing for the Curtain

Now I can speak out clearly with confidence. I was not wrong. Perhaps I failed, but I was not wrong. My failure is no cause for regret. Because I have not particularly gone on living for the conclusion.

I hear the sound of the front door shutting.

She has gone. At this point I am neither angry nor bitter. The sound of the door closing was filled with deep sympathy and compassion. There was no enmity or strife between us. I imagine that even she, if it were possible, would have wished to disappear without using the front door. Thus she was hesitant about slamming it. After waiting ten minutes I shall nail up the door. I don't really expect her back. I shall simply wait until she gets far enough away so that she will not hear the sound of hammering.

When I finish with the entrance, there only remains the lock on the door of the emergency stairs on the second floor. As the windows and vents are securely blocked with plywood or cardboard, there is no place for the sunlight to enter during the day. This is all the more true now on this overcast evening. The whole building is entirely cut off from the outside world, and there are neither entrances nor exits. After seeing to this, I leave. It is an escape of which only a box man is capable. As for where I escape to and by what means, I intend to write about that last of all in these notes.

A ten-minute lapse.

Now I have just nailed up the entrance. My aim was off, and I grazed the base of the nail of my left thumb. A little blood seeped out, but the pain went away at once.

When I think about it, we did not after all exchange a single word from the time I returned from outside to when she left. I had some regret. But I imagined that the regret would not vanish just by having talked with her. The stage where words were useful had already passed. By just exchanging glances we already understood each other. This too-complete communication was a phenomenon that appeared in the process of our disintegrating love.

Her expression was a little tense. Or perhaps it just looked that way because of the light makeup. Anyway the change of expression was of little importance to me, being merely a small part of the change in her. The important thing was that she was dressed. What the clothing was was scarcely the question at this juncture. For close to two months she had been living naked. I, too, in my box, was naked. At home we were naked together. And except for us there was nobody there. We had taken off the name plate and the sign from the door and turned out the red lamp at the gate, and even callers who stopped in by mistake completely ceased coming. There was no need even to put out the sign canceling examinations.

Once a day I would put on the box and go out into the town. Wandering about the streets like a transparent person, I would go around collecting miscellaneous items for daily use, principally foodstuffs. If I did not go into a given store more than once a month, I had no worry about being challenged. We could not live high on the hog, but we also didn't lack any comforts. I was confident that if there were just the two of us, we could go on living like this for any number of years.

When I would come up the back emergency stairs and take off my boots and box in the corridor on the second floor, she would be waiting for me and come running up from below. This was the most exciting moment in the whole day. I would always get an erection, though for a short while. Swaying, we would hug each other so closely there was not a sliver of space between us. However, our vocabulary was comically poor. Her head came just to my nose, and when I would murmur how fragrant her hair smelled, she would follow up with how smooth and round my buttocks were, giving them a succession of little pats. But I hardly think that's the point. The efficacy of words extends up to a line eight feet away, at which point one can distinguish the other person clearly as different. Nor could I imagine that the morgue by the stairway would cast its shadow between the two of us. We had decided to ignore it completely, and when we did the room was in fact nonexistent.

After some minutes, at about the time my erection was going down, we at length broke our embrace and turned toward the kitchen at the end of the corridor. Even though we had separated, we always kept our bodies in contact. For example, while she was peeling potatoes or chopping leeks at the sink, I would sit at her feet and slowly keep passing my hand over her legs. Mold was growing faintly on the kitchen floor. The real kitchen was downstairs, and this one was neglected, almost unused; it had been set up previously for the inpatients of the hospital. That was the only reason why we began using this one. There was an empty room across the corridor where it was convenient to pile up the kitchen wastes. Old vegetables, fish heads, and similar things were temporarily kept in plastic bags, but the mice broke into them for food, and the contents lay scattered everywhere on the floor. After a half day they began to rot, and a clinging stench spilled out every time the door was opened and closed. We took no notice of that. For one thing, when you're touching skin with someone else it seems that your sense of smell undergoes a transformation. And then too perhaps we sensed without realizing it that it provided a good opportunity to forget the existence of the morgue. We talked only about our optimistic estimate that it would take at least half a year to fill up the room with garbage.

But was it in fact optimistic? I think we had simply abandoned hope from the beginning. Passion is the urge to burn oneself out. Perhaps we were only too much in a hurry to burn ourselves out. We were afraid of our love stopping before burning out, but we were not sure we wanted to go on the way people usually do. We could not imagine things as far as a half year in the future, when the room would be full of garbage. We continued touching one part or another of each other's bodies the whole day long. We rarely went out of a circle eight feet in diameter. At that distance the other person could almost not be seen, but we didn't consider that particularly inconvenient. If in our imaginations we connected the various parts of ourselves together, we had the feeling of actually seeing each other, and more than that our sense of liberation at not being seen by the other one was great. I dissolved into parts in front of her. Other than her comments on the feel of my buttocks, she gave absolutely no voice to any opinion touching my whole personality . . . whether she liked it or whether she abhorred it. That didn't particularly bother me. Words themselves had already begun to lose their meaning. Time had stopped.

Three days, three weeks, were all the same. No matter how long our love goes on burning, when it is burnt out it is over in an instant.

Thus when I noticed that instead of a naked girl running up, the one today was dressed and looking up at me in silence, I was not particularly nonplused and was able to manage merely experiencing a little disappointment, as if returning to the starting point. But my own nakedness seemed terribly piteous. As if sent away, I returned to my box, and there was nothing to do but to wait motionlessly for her to leave. She frowned and looked around, but pretended not to take notice of me. She seemed only to be trying to identify the source of the stench. She slowly looked over her shoulder and then withdrew to her own room. Muffling my steps, I too returned to the former examination room. If this was the starting point, would we be successful commencing all over again from the beginning? Of course, it should be possible to start over again any number of times. Straining my ears, I listened for her out in the corridor. There was no sign of her moving. Could she be waiting for me to suggest starting over again? But no matter how many times we began again, the same time, the same place would simply repeat.

The dial of the clock wears out unevenly;
Most worn
Is the area round eight.
As it is stared at with abrasive glances
unfailingly twice a day,
It is weathered away.
On the other side

The area at two
Is only half as worn,
For closed eyes at night
Pass without stopping.
If there is one who possesses a flat watch evenly
     worn,
It is he who, failing at the start, is running
     one lap behind.

Thus the world is always
A lap fast—
The world he thinks he sees
Has not yet begun.
Illusory time,
When the hands stand vertically on the dial;
Without the bell announcing the raising of the
     curtain,
The play has come to an end.

.   .   .

And now my last confession. I actually heard the noise of
the door to her room. I could not have heard the front door.
That has been nailed up from the first. It had been the most
trouble and was firmly closed off. She cannot get out that
way. The emergency stairs are locked; she has to be confined
within the building now. Only that confounded blouse and
skirt are separating her from me. But if I cut off the electricity the effect of her clothes too will end. If she cannot be
seen, that will be the same as her being naked. I can't stand
being seen by her when she is wearing clothes. In the dark-

ness it's the same as being with a blind man. She will again become gentle. I am completely liberated from the need to wrack my brains for some uninviting plan to gouge out her eyes or anything like that.

Instead of leaving the box, I shall enclose the world within it. Now the world must have closed its eyes. Things will definitely go the way I wish. In the building articles such as matches, candles, lighters, to say nothing of my flashlight, anything that creates shadows or form has been disposed of.

After a time, I cut the power. I looked in at her room, not purposely making myself conspicuous, but not especially stealthily either. Of course, I have taken off the box and am naked. I expected only faint signs of her in the depths of the darkness and was astounded at the unexpected change in the room. There was much too much discrepancy with what I had expected. I was more greatly perplexed than surprised. The space that was supposed to be a room had changed into an alleyway, like one behind shops, adjoining some station. Across the alley from the shops stood a building with a real estate office combined with a privately run baggage room. It was a narrow alley barely large enough to let a person by, and even without any special knowledge of the place one could at once assume from the topography and the direction that it was a dead-end alley cut off by the precincts of some station. Except to urinate, no one would be entering.

The passage was blocked by bundles of rubber hose, an incinerator made from a metal drum, cardboard boxes piled up, and a line of about five bowls of bonsai that had begun to dry out, mixed in with old bicycles. For what purpose, I wondered, had she lost herself in such a place? Even supposing her objective was to find cardboard, did she intend to steal out of here and go somewhere?

When I went ahead, treading my way through the trash, I came to a narrow little stairway in concrete just where it seemed to be a dead end. It was not very steep and was about five steps high. When I reached the bottom, it was hard to believe, but a sturdy concrete balcony jutted out. One could at once infer that the plans for an overpass had altered during the course of construction and that it had been abandoned in its present state.

I went down to the balcony. Suddenly the wind strengthened, and the sounds of night construction on the railroad sighed in the distance. The sky was tinged a reddish purple, doubtless the reflection against the clouds of the neon lights in the streets. I took another step, and suddenly right before me there was nothing, and I could see the roadbed twenty or twenty-five feet below. I had the feeling of being in a construction elevator suspended in the skeleton of an unfinished building and between two concrete walls that were shedding tears like bird droppings.

I must find her. But there is no place further to advance from here. This is a part of closed space after all. Nevertheless, where could she have vanished to? Gingerly I looked down, but it was dark and I could see nothing. If I tried taking another step further, what would happen? I was curious. But I supposed I would be no closer to finding her. Anyway the whole thing was simply taking place in the same building.

Oh, yes, before I forget, one more important addition. In processing the box the most important thing in all events is to ensure leaving plenty of blank space for scribbling. No, there'll always be plenty of blank space. No matter how assiduous one is in scribbling, one can never cover all the blank space. It always surprises me, but scribbling of a certain type is blank itself. At least there'll always remain enough space to write one's name in. But if you don't wish to believe even that, it doesn't make the slightest difference.

Actually a box, in appearance, is purely and simply a right-angled parallelepiped, but when you look at it from within it's a labyrinth of a hundred interconnecting puzzle rings. The more you struggle the more the box, like an extra outer skin growing from the body, creates new twists for the labyrinth, making the inner disposition increasingly more complex.

One thing alone is certain and that is that even she, who has at present vanished, is hiding somewhere in this labyrinth. She's not necessarily running away, she just can't find where I am. At this point I can speak out clearly with assurance. I have no regret. The clues are numerous, and it is reasonable that the truth should exist in proportion to their number.

I hear the siren of an approaching ambulance.

A Note About the Author

Kobo Abé was born in Tokyo in 1924 but grew up in Mukden, Manchuria, where his father, a doctor, was on the staff of the medical school. As a young man Mr. Abé was interested in mathematics and insect collecting, as well as the works of Poe, Dostoevsky, Nietzsche, Heidegger, Jaspers, and Kafka. He received a medical degree from Tokyo University in 1948, but he has never practiced medicine. In that same year he published his first book, *The Road Sign at the End of the Street*. In 1951 he was awarded the most important Japanese literary prize, the Akutagawa, for his novella *The Crime of Mr. S. Karuma*. In 1960 his novel *The Woman in the Dunes* won the Yomiuri Prize for Literature. It was made into a film by Hiroshi Teshigahara in 1963 and won the Jury Prize at the Cannes Film Festival, and was the first of Mr. Abé's novels to be published in translation in the United States (1964). *The Face of Another* (1966) was also made into a film by Mr. Teshigahara. Most recently published here were his novels *The Ruined Map* (1969) and *Inter Ice Age 4* (1970). Mr. Abé lives with his wife, Machi, an artist, on the outskirts of Tokyo.

A Note About the Translator

E. Dale Saunders, translator of Kobo Abé's *The Woman in the Dunes* (1964), *The Face of Another* (1966), *The Ruined Map* (1969), and *Inter Ice Age 4* (1970), received his A.B. from Western Reserve University (1941), his M.A. from Harvard (1948), and his Ph.D. from the University of Paris (1952). He is Professor of Japanese at the University of Pennsylvania and has also taught at International Christian University, Tokyo, and at Harvard University. Among his publications are *Mudrā: A Study of Symbolic Gestures in Japanese Buddhist Sculpture* (1960) and *Buddhism in Japan* (1964).